SECRETS: BLUEGRASS HOMECOMING

BOOKS 1 & 2

JAN SCARBROUGH

SADDLE HORSE PRESS

Copyright © 2016 Jan Scarbrough
Scarbrough, Jan
Secrets: Bluegrass Homecoming
Media > Books > Fiction > Romance Novels
Category/Tags: second chances, secret baby, wedding, seasoned romance,
contemporary women, later in life

Print ISBN: 978-0997191981

Saddle Horse Press Digital release: December, 2016

Edited by Karen Block
Cover Design by Kim Jacobs

This edition is published by agreement with Saddle Horse Press, PO Box 221543,
Louisville, KY 40252.

I

PREQUEL: BLUEGRASS HOMECOMING

Grace Baron had always been the good wife, in spite of a marriage based on a careless indiscretion, and sustained not by love, but by old-fashioned morality. She'd raised her daughter, bit her tongue, and silently lived with her guilt. Now that she's a widow, she can't help being glad for her sudden freedom. She'd never live her life like that again. Without a sense of control. Without deliberately making a choice about her future. And that future would never involve getting married again.

Small town lawyer Howard Scott has buried two wives. His steadfast belief that it's never too late to find true love keeps him open to whatever joy life has to offer. He doesn't want another socialite wife. This time he wants a hometown girl. Someone stable, maybe a little naïve, but feisty enough to keep him on his toes. Someone like Grace Baron.

Howard's gentle, old-fashioned courting makes Grace feel alive again. Would marrying Howard be the trap Grace fears, or would it finally give her a kind of freedom she'd never imagined?

CHAPTER ONE

"I've buried two wives," the man said. "I miss them. I'm not good living alone."

Grace Baron pressed her lips into a tight line, and her gaze flitted from the only man in the circle to the three other widows. They'd all been left behind to cope, just as she had. They weren't doing well, it seemed, by the looks of them, especially a young woman sitting next to her crying and dabbing her eyes with a tissue. She couldn't stop the tears. Her grief consumed her.

Was there something wrong with her? Why didn't she miss her husband of almost forty years? In fact, in her heart of hearts, she was glad for the sudden freedom. She'd always been somebody's wife and mother, defined by those roles. All she wanted now was to live a little in the time left her.

There was only one problem—she didn't know *how* to live.

She didn't know herself—her wants, her likes. Being submissive to her husband in an old school way, she'd never explored the world. Herself. Her grief came more from regret, not sorrow. And guilt. She had a lot of that—from her mistakes as a young woman to those she'd made with her only daughter. And a big part of her was sad she'd never stood up for herself. Never had the courage, the courage she'd somehow given her daughter.

"Do you know how you're going to handle your grief, Howard?" June Hobson asked.

June was the volunteer who ran the support group and Grace's childhood friend, a friendship that had suffered during her marriage. The church didn't have a trained professional, but June had lost her husband almost fifteen years earlier. She'd seen this grief support group as her calling. Helping others, she'd said, had brought her out of her heartache. So, it had been natural for June to reach out to Grace when her husband died, draw her back to church, and into the group for support.

It had taken more than a year before Grace had felt comfortable enough to join. But here she was, her first day in the group—wide-eyed, cautious, and mouth shut.

"In my opinion, it's never too late to find true love," Howard answered. He was serious. His blue eyes stared pointedly at June. "I plan to marry again."

The young woman next to Grace gasped. "How can you? Isn't that disloyal to your wife's memory?"

"I cherish the memory of both my wives," he said, calmly pointing out he was not new to remarrying. "They both gave me love. One gave me a son. But they are gone now, and I am not."

It seemed so simple for this man, but it was an option Grace found awful.

"I will never marry again," Grace said in a quiet tone. All eyes turned to her

"And why is that, Grace?" June asked.

"I don't trust love."

How could she? Not after what she'd gone through being married all those years to Lee Baron.

"But you love your daughter," June observed.

Grace lowered her eyes and stared at her hands. She hadn't made herself clear. The inability to communicate had been one of her problems during her marriage. She looked up at the members of the group. "Between a husband and wife," she clarified.

The room was silent. Only the quiet sobs of the woman sitting next to Grace broke the stillness.

"That's the saddest thing I've heard all day," Howard finally said in his deep baritone voice.

Grace lifted her gaze to meet his compassionate one. She knew this man. How could she not know the former mayor of Heritage Springs and a prominent town lawyer? They'd never personally met, never been in the same social circles, but Howard Scott was well known to everyone in the small community.

As they stared at each other, Grace became defensive. What right did he have to judge her? She'd lived her life the best she knew how. She'd been loyal, accepting the consequences of her actions. Pleasing her parents, her husband. In the end, she'd not pleased her daughter and lost her, but she'd made her choices for reasons she thought moral.

Raising her chin and tilting back her head, Grace refused to buckle under the man's scrutiny. She'd spent her life doing that. Never again. No, never again.

~

"MRS. BARON, WAIT!"

Grace paused at the church door, turned, and watched Howard Scott hurry toward her.

He came to a halt, towering over her. "Mrs. Baron, I'm afraid I hurt your feelings."

"Why?" His presence unnerved her. She rarely spoke to a man alone except for the grocer behind the checkout counter or the clerk at the cleaners.

He lowered his head, his gaze seeming to devour her face, sweep across her body and return to her eyes. She shifted her stance, his direct inspection making her uncomfortable. "It was presumptuous of me to comment on your remark, especially since I know nothing of your circumstances," he said.

Well, it had been rude. And there had been nothing she wanted to do more than snap back a sarcastic reply, but she was unable to open her mouth to say so. Too many years of biting her tongue, keeping silent, lay between her and this man who had come to apologize.

In the silence, Howard ran a hand through his gray hair. He had plenty of it for a man his age. Not like Lee who'd lost his brown hair early and wore an ill-fitting toupee, as if that could effectively hide the bald spot on his head.

"The thing is, we're supposed to open up in the group," Howard went on. "I'm simply used to speaking what's on my mind in there." He smiled, as if at a private joke. "As a lawyer, too much of my life has been spent watching what I say, choosing my words in front of a judge or client. I enjoy the grief support group. It gives me a chance to say what's on my mind. I hope you come to enjoy it too."

That was the most a man had said to her in years. The sincerity on his face and the kindness in his voice overwhelmed her.

Grace searched his eyes. The crow's feet at the corners were like hers, there because of age. He had wrinkles that were hard to hide—on his brow, at the sides of his lips. She dropped her eyes quickly, ashamed of staring at his face. "I want to thank you for apologizing," she said.

"I want to thank you for being so understanding."

Looking up again, Grace caught his smile. It was a pleasant smile, without the smirk she had so often seen on her husband's face.

Taken aback, Grace turned away and reached for the door handle. Howard stepped forward, beating her to the handle, and pushed the massive front door open. Standing aside, he let her pass through into the gray February afternoon. His gallantry disconcerted her more than anything, and she rushed down the steps as if she couldn't get away fast enough.

He followed her. "May I see you to your car?"

"I walked." Grace glanced up at him. He was a tall man, lithe and muscular. He appeared to keep himself in shape. She felt tiny beside him. "I live up the hill from the square."

"I see," he said. "Then I'll walk you home."

"There's no need."

"But I want to."

He fell into step beside her, measuring his strides to hers. Surprised by his chivalry, Grace tried to swallow her bashfulness. What was she supposed to say to this man? How was she to act?

"I don't have a car," she admitted. That was a point of conversation, perhaps.

"If you live near the square, you probably have little need of one," he said. "I bet walking keeps you in shape. No need for the gym and boring exercises."

"No, I don't go to a gym." In fact, the climb up the cracked sidewalk from Heritage Springs' historic downtown square hardly winded her.

"Not many people our age are as healthy as we," Howard commented. "Many people can't take a walk like this."

"Really?" She'd never considered it. In fact, she'd never considered much of anything about her age or state of life, not until Lee dropped dead of a heart attack. Then she'd confronted the fact she was nothing without being Mrs. Lee Baron. Marriage had done that to her.

No. She had done it to herself. Trapped in a loveless marriage, she'd withered away, letting the person she had always wanted to become die a long, slow death.

They soon reached Grace's two-story frame house with its wraparound front porch. The house was white, just like the picket fence surrounding it. Lee's grandfather had built it in 1909. An old-fashioned porch swing suspended immobile from the ceiling joists. This was home. It was her only inheritance from the man she'd devoted so many years to. She supposed she loved the house. At the very least, she was used to it.

They paused at the gate. "This is lovely," Howard said.

"I guess."

"I'm sure its location makes it worth a lot of money."

Grace shrugged. "I hadn't thought about that." What was she supposed to do with this man now that she'd reached her destination?

He must have read her mind. "I won't keep you," he told her. "I needed the walk, and accompanying you was a perfect excuse to get outside. We've had a warm winter."

"Yes." Grace gazed up at him. She put her hand on the gate.

There was a hesitation. A pregnant pause. What were they both waiting for? She didn't know what to say or do. Did he expect her to invite him inside?

"May I ask you something, Mrs. Baron?"

"Grace." There was no reason for him to be so formal.

"Grace." He smiled down at her, a comforting, gentle smile.

Grace felt her heart stutter in her chest.

"I was wondering, Grace, if you would accompany me to a dinner next weekend in Louisville."

She drew a sharp breath. "Me?"

"Yes." He rushed on. "You don't have to decide right now. It's a week from this Saturday. You can tell me next week at the support group."

"I told you, Mr. Scott…"

"Please call me Howard."

Grace flashed a wry smile and started again. "I told you, Howard, that I have no intention of marrying again. If you think to invite me on a date simply to coax me into changing my mind, you are sorely mistaken." When had she ever spoken so bluntly to a man? She felt a rush of heat on her cheeks.

And he laughed. He had the audacity to laugh at her. Her cheeks flamed now with indignation.

"Oh, Grace, you are so delightful! You are exactly the woman I need to go with me, and yes, it is a date of sorts. But you will be my protector. Having you with me will discourage other women. Being an eligible bachelor at my age is very difficult, you see."

She didn't see. "I don't understand."

Howard's expression softened, and he spoke in a slow, serious voice. "I have no ulterior motives. I simply need you to be by my side at this dinner. I often have to fend off gold diggers. I'm tired of it. A woman who knows her mind, who's comfortable in her own skin, is refreshing."

Was that how he saw her? Grace hardly recognized the woman he described. It confused her. She didn't know how to react.

He must have seen her hesitation. He clasped her hand. "As I said, you don't have to answer me now. Let me know next week, will you?"

"Yes," she said, sounding breathy even to her own ears. "I'll let you know."

"Good!" He squeezed her hand again. "Until then."

Howard turned on his heel and strode down the sidewalk toward the square like a man who'd just won a victory.

Slowly, Grace raised the hand he had held and touched her lips with it. What had happened to her? What was this turmoil spinning in her stomach? And what in the hell would she tell Heritage Springs' former mayor when she saw him again?

CHAPTER TWO

The next morning, after a sleepless night, Grace pulled on her coat, picked up a loaf of homemade banana bread, and crossed the street to have tea with June Hobson. Over the years, June had often invited her for morning tea, but until Lee passed, Grace had not taken her up on the invitation. Now she looked forward to it, meeting the other widow at least twice a week to share recipes and a bit of small town gossip.

Discussing the grief support group would bend the rules. What happened in support group stayed in support group, didn't it?

But what happened *after* support group was fair game for discussion.

"I was so surprised," Grace said after telling June about her walk home the previous day. "I didn't know what to say." She stirred half-and-half into her cup of Earl Gray tea, trying to act nonchalant. She hadn't discussed an eligible man with another woman in what seemed like a lifetime.

"Oh, my!" June didn't seem to know what to say either.

"Why did he single me out? I've just joined the group."

June brought her cup of tea up to her lips, sipped it, and set it down in the saucer. "I swear, I have no clue," she said. "He was telling the truth about the gold diggers. I've seen widows, and even married women, throw themselves at him. It's got to be disconcerting."

"To say the least." Grace tasted her tea. Whatever his reasons, she felt flattered.

"Maybe it's because you're a new member in the group. He doesn't know you."

"That's true."

"You know men, at least men our age, like to pursue a woman. In our day, we weren't as forward as women today, even though women were becoming liberated and burning bras. In a small town, it was different. I remember many nights waiting patiently by the phone for Peter to call me." June sighed and glanced at a portrait of her departed husband. "It never crossed my mind to pick up the phone and dial him."

Grace had to smile. "That was when we still had to dial a phone number. We had landlines and no one had ever heard of a cell phone."

June nodded. "It's a new age. I'm not sure I like it."

"I'm not sure either," Grace agreed as she sipped her tea, losing herself in her thoughts.

Years ago, almost forty years, Grace had waited for Lee to call. She'd been patient. And when he did call, when he did take her out, she was so into pleasing him, enthralled by the whole experience of having a boy like her, that she did things without thinking of the consequences. She'd lived with those consequences until the day he died. The sad part was she'd never been able to right the wrong. Nothing was ever good enough for Lee. Nothing made up for one mistake. Instead, that slip-up seemed to magnify year by year, and as she lost control of her life and then her daughter, she'd fallen deeper into despair.

She'd never told anyone—not her daughter Kelly, not June—but after Lee's death, she'd spent a lot of time coming to grips with her life. After marriage and Kelly's birth, Grace had become dependent, relying on Lee for everything, afraid to make a move without his approval. That's the way she'd been brought up by highly religious parents with strict views on a woman's place in marriage. She behaved as a wife should behave.

Slowly, over the past year, she'd broken free of the *shoulds* that had restrained her for so many years. Before, she would never have considered going anywhere without Lee. Now she was able to visit June for tea and go to the church support group. Baby steps. She was changing. Maybe not fast enough, but at her own pace. In her own mind.

"I believe you should accept his invitation," June said, then nodded her head as if she liked the idea. "You've told me you want to get out more. What better opportunity could you have but to go to dinner with Howard Scott?"

Grace let June's suggestion roll around in her head. Her stomach felt awash in acid. Why was she so frightened? Unlike Lee, Howard was a big man. Imposing. Did that scare her? He was also courteous and kind. And again unlike Lee, he'd treated her with respect. Even though she'd made it clear she wanted nothing from him, he said he only wanted her companionship. What was so scary about that?

Or was she afraid of herself? Of the stirrings of womanhood he'd awakened in their short walk home? Good grief. Even admitting that scared her, causing a sharp pain in her stomach. But she'd been fearful most of her life. She was tired of it. Tired of being a mouse. Tired of playing the good wife. She'd proven she could be one, that's for sure, but at what cost? Her own selfhood. Odd that she'd realized it so late in life. But thank God, she had finally come to her senses.

"Going to dinner doesn't mean more than that," she told June.

"It doesn't mean you're going to marry the man," June agreed.

"Heavens, no! I'm tired of taking care of a grouchy old man."

"Exactly!"

Grace took a bite of banana bread and chewed it slowly. Swallowing it, and then taking a deep breath, she gave June a tiny smile. "Okay, then. I'll accept his invitation."

"Good for you!"

That decision made, Grace realized she had another problem. "What in the hell am I going to wear?"

"You ought to remarry, son," Howard Scott said. He removed the lime garnish from his glass and sipped his margarita, all the while staring at a younger version of himself.

Wednesday evening was their regular night out for dinner. They usually stuck pretty close to home, preferring the Tex-Mex cuisine at the local restaurant on the square. His son was divorced, unhappily so. He'd give anything to see Rob happy again.

Rob dipped a corn chip into the bowl of salsa and waved the chip at his father. "I'm not eager to try a second time."

"I don't know why. It's never too late to find true love."

"It's different for you, Dad. Both your wives died. Mine left me for another man."

"And I say good riddance too."

Howard could tell Rob didn't agree, but he needed to get over that sentiment. That cheating wife of his was no good for him. His son needed to start over again. *Don't look back*, Howard always said to himself. *You're not going that way.*

"It's been two years since the last Mrs. Scott died," Rob pointed out between bites of chips and dip. "I'd say you're slipping, old man. Why haven't you married again?"

Howard scoffed at his son's remark. "Have you seen the pickings in this town lately? A man my age has few good-looking women to choose from."

Rob frowned, deriding his father's observation. "What about a younger woman?"

"Now why would I want to rob the cradle?" Howard sipped his drink. "Most younger women are only after one thing." He paused dramatically, lifting his eyebrows for effect. "My body."

Rob laughed. "More likely they're after your money."

"I can tell you don't know how hard it is to be rich *and* handsome."

Poking fun at each other was a family tradition. From the time Rob had been little, Howard had played with him, kidded him, perhaps as a way to counteract the seriousness of his first wife, Rob's over-critical mother. Now, *she'd* been a woman impressed by her social position in their small Kentucky county seat, controlling their married life as if she was running the communication office in the White House.

Fearing another social climber, Howard had gone to Louisville to select his second wife, a woman who turned out to hate small town life. Their marriage had been amicable until the end, but she'd never been happy in Heritage Springs. He had sensed this discontent but always remained at a loss about how to change it.

The waitress brought two beef and bean burritos drenched in enchilada sauce, placed one in front of each man, and all conversation ceased while they dug into their meal.

Tomorrow was the weekly grief support group at church. Grace had promised to let him know if she'd go to dinner. Howard hoped she'd say yes. Memories of her charming authenticity had preoccupied him all week. Time had aged her, but just enough to highlight her mature beauty. There was elegance about her, a quiet reserve that he liked.

Finishing with his meal, Howard wiped his lips with a napkin and surveyed his son. Rob had taken over his law firm, just as he'd hoped. It was too bad his son didn't have his own son to carry on the family tradition. His wife had not wanted children. Howard figured that had been the greatest disappointment of Rob's life— until the divorce, of course.

"I have a likely candidate for the next Mrs. Scott," Howard revealed at last.

Rob perked up. "Well, that's more like it."

"I met her at the support group last week. She's a widow too."

"You seem to like widows."

"Tried and tested," Howard acknowledged with a nod of irony. Then he smiled remembering Grace's reluctance to walk with him.

"It's strange I've never met her before. She's lived in town all her life. She doesn't care who I am. She's not a social climber."

"Who is the paragon of virtue?"

Howard smiled again remembering her name. He hoped it wasn't a silly smile, one inappropriate for a man of his advancing age. "Her name is Grace Baron."

Rob almost choked on his glass of ice water. "Kelly's mother?"

"I'm not sure. We haven't conversed long enough to discuss the names of children. Why? Do you know Grace?"

His son looked a shade paler, almost as if he'd seen a ghost. "I knew a Kelly Baron in high school."

"Grace lives in a white house on Main Street."

"That's the same family." Rob sat forward and put his elbows on the table. "Kelly's father was a real SOB. I felt sorry for her. And her mother seemed under the man's thumb as well."

Howard shrugged. "The man is dead and gone. I doubt he can control Grace from the grave."

He could tell he'd thrown his son for a loop by mentioning Grace. Or was it the daughter? Perhaps it was too soon to confide in him, just as it was perhaps too soon to dream again. But he was lonely, dammit. He was only sixty-six. He wanted to remarry. And Grace was a lovely woman who knew her own mind. She intrigued him. Finding her after two years of living alone was a godsend.

Rob had pulled himself together and reached for the tab. "My turn tonight, Dad."

"I'll let you. Turnabout is fair play."

Reaching for his wallet, Rob shook his head as if expressing disapproval. "You know something? For a smart lawyer, a former mayor, and a heck of a good man, you are still damn crazy."

Howard laughed, throwing back his head. *God, how I love this boy.* It's too bad his son's marriage had not given him a child.

"You know what they say, son?" He gave Rob a pointed look. "An apple never falls far from the tree."

CHAPTER THREE

Dinner was held in a private Louisville home. Grace had no idea where it was located, except it was on the east side of the city. The hour-long drive from Heritage Springs in Howard's silver Lexus SUV with its fancy leather interior had been pleasant. Howard's music system played a nostalgic mix of fifties and sixties pop such as Frank Sinatra and Nat King Cole and even early rock and roll recordings.

She'd been shy when Howard came to her house to pick her up. Coming up with something to say proved difficult. Thank goodness listening to the music meant she didn't have to carry on a conversation. Why had she agreed to this torture? Shouldn't she be home in her pajamas and woolen socks?

But she wasn't. And when Howard opened the car door for her at their destination, she stepped out into the cold night air feeling like a queen arriving at court.

He took her hand, as if to give her confidence, and fell into step beside her as they walked the paved sidewalk to the front door. It opened immediately to a white-coated servant and the glare of bright lights and sound of shrill laughter.

"These are my business partners," Howard said, leaning down to whisper in her ear. "Relax and have a good time."

Easy for him to say. He's from this world.

In the vestibule, the waiter took their coats and her purse. As soon as they walked into the formal living room, they were immediately swept into the festivities. The atmosphere was electric. Loud. Intense. Two women sat on gray facing sofas in front of an ornate fireplace, its fire blazing. A cluster of men, deep in conversation, stood in front of a large floor-to-ceiling oil painting of vibrant reds and blues.

Another white-coated waiter approached and silently offered a tray of crystal goblets filled with wine.

"Red or white?" Howard asked.

Grace swallowed hard. Lee didn't allow alcohol in the house, but he was not here. She tipped her head, took another breath and answered, "Red, if you please."

With something in her hands, she didn't feel defenseless. That was a welcome relief.

Howard also took a glass of red wine, held it up to her in a silent toast, and smiled at her over the rim as he took his first sip. Grace felt her eyes grow wide with wonder, pleased by his attention. She returned his salute with a nod and small smile. Then she took her first sip.

A woman approached dressed in a silver cocktail dress with a draped neckline showing off her perfect pale skin. Her hair was artificially silver, piled in a bouffant style reminiscent of the nineteen sixties. She wore strappy heels and was almost as tall as Howard.

Grace couldn't help wondering how many facelifts the woman had undergone, and for once, she was not a bit concerned about her unkind thoughts.

"My gracious, Howard Scott, I thought you'd never arrive!"

"I'm here now, Margeaux," Howard said with a friendly grin.

Margeaux grasped Howard's shoulders, puckered, and kissed the air near both his cheeks one right after the other. Grace had seen that sort of affectation done on television, usually by Europeans, but never in real life.

"Margeaux Smithson, may I introduce you to my date, Grace Baron?"

Date? Grace glanced at Howard and then at the silver-haired woman. She transferred her glass to her left hand and offered her right to the hostess. "How do you do?"

Margeaux took hers in an imitation of a handshake. It was limp, hardly worth doing. Yet her gaze was anything but lifeless. Speculation sprang in the hostess' eyes as she gave Grace a good, hard look. Then she dismissed her almost as soon as she let her hand slip from Grace's grasp. The obvious nature of the woman's disregard was almost amusing if it wasn't so rude. Wasn't Grace enough of a threat?

Turning her attention totally to Howard, Margeaux caught his arm. "Come in, dear. You haven't seen the Bradfords or Drakes for months. Or us either. Where have you been keeping yourself?"

But Howard wouldn't leave Grace behind. He dislodged himself from Margeaux's grip and turned back to Grace. "Come meet the whole team," he said, holding his hand out to her.

Grace caught it and allowed herself to be drawn forward alongside Howard. After being introduced first to the gentlemen, Grace found herself sitting beside Sissy Bradford and facing Candice Drake, who sat on the opposite sofa.

Margeaux Smithson flitted around the room, like a bird afraid to light, not a bit interested in socializing with the wives. Her husband appeared to be the oldest of the four men, maybe nearing eighty. He certainly had wed a significantly younger woman. She was perhaps in her very early sixties.

"You must tell us your secret, Grace, honey," Mrs. Bradford said, leaning toward Grace.

"My secret?"

"Howard hasn't brought a date to one of these functions in over a year," she whispered. "Not since that last disaster with a forty-something woman who was definitely after his money."

So that is why Howard wants me for protection.

Glad for the security of the glass in her hand, Grace took a sip of wine. How should she respond to the inquiry? She hardly knew Howard Scott.

"Oh, Sissy, don't be so forward," Candice said in a scolding hiss. "Grace isn't interested in our tittle-tattle."

"Well, she must have done something to catch Howard's fastidious eye."

Good grief.

What had she gotten herself into? Was she a pawn in a game she knew nothing about? She felt terribly out of her league.

Suddenly, Grace longed to be home in her pajamas. But as she took a deep breath and another sip of wine, she reminded herself of her own ulterior motive. She'd spent years at home in her pajamas reading books and living other people's lives vicariously. It was time to live her own life, and if her presence helped Howard in some way, she was glad to assist. After all, he'd shared his heartache in the safety of the support group. She seriously doubted he'd ever spoken his true feelings to this group of so-called friends.

As HE NURSED his glass of wine, Howard kept a close eye on Grace. She seemed to be holding her own with the ladies. He liked that. It also tickled him to have annoyed Margeaux by bringing a date. He'd guessed right, realizing six months ago he was part of Margeaux's future playbook. As soon as Bob Smithson died, his widow would make herself the number one candidate to be the new Mrs. Scott.

But Howard had other ideas. He didn't want another socialite wife like his first two. He wanted a hometown girl. Stable. Maybe a little naïve, but feisty enough to keep him on his toes. He saw that kind of woman in Grace Baron. He longed to know her better.

"She's an attractive woman, Howard," his host said.

The other men had drifted away, deep into a political argument. Bob had evidently noticed where Howard directed his riveted gaze.

Caught red-handed Howard grinned into his wine glass then took a sip. He was self-conscious about his reply. "She is, isn't she? Grace has lived in Heritage Springs all her life, but as small as that town is, I never met her until last week."

"Then it was meant to be," Bob observed. "I believe things happen in their own time."

"Yes, perhaps you're right."

His partner's philosophical musing grabbed Howard's attention. He liked the *meant to be* part. It solidified his own thinking in a way he'd not yet mentally verbalized, even to himself.

Margeaux came up cooing about dinner being ready and drew Bob away, leaving Howard standing in front of the oil painting for a moment. The oil was a riot of color, like Grace's simple, but bright cocktail dress. She wore it well, with an elegance he hadn't expected. As he watched her chatting with the wives, he was drawn even more to her petite beauty.

They might be old, but they weren't yet in a nursing home. There was plenty of spirit left in both of them, and Howard was determined to take advantage of it all.

DINNER WAS SOON SERVED in a formal dining room. The table accommodated eight and was completed by parsons chairs upholstered in a yellow, blue and rust fabric. Grace didn't talk much as she ate a dinner of herb-roasted salmon, grilled asparagus, and classic Caesar salad. A bottle of Pinot Grigio was paired with the salmon. Nice and light, but still fruity and fragrant. Grace found herself sipping her second glass of wine that evening, suddenly feeling untroubled and a little giddy.

She listened with interest to the conversation. The discussion around the table was fascinating. For one thing, she learned these "partners" of Howard's were a horse racing syndicate. The four families owned three Thoroughbred horses, two of them in training.

Talk of running their horses at Keeneland in the spring and even during the undercard on Kentucky Derby day, the first Saturday in May, sounded exciting. The syndicate's horses weren't major stakes winners, but they weren't claimers either. The partnership had good money tied up in the venture, and splitting the cost made it doable for each one. They were enthusiastic, but maintained, what seemed to Grace, a realistic view of their prospects. No Derby winners in their stable, she heard them say, but one mare was in foal to the industry's leading sire. They had high hopes. Maybe, this foal, due any day now, would be the one—their "big" horse—their Triple Crown champion.

Grace admired Howard even more because, not only did he have big dreams, but he also did something to make them a reality unlike Lee, who never dreamed, never wanted anything more in his life than his comfortable job and traditionally strict household.

"Thank you for coming with me," Howard said later that night while handing her into his Lexus for the return ride home.

Grace settled into the comfortable leather seat. When he climbed into the driver's side, she turned to him and said, "I enjoyed myself. Thank you for inviting me."

"It was my pleasure, Grace." He gazed at her a moment, and then added, "Truly."

Heat flushed her face. She was glad for the darkness. Her gaze searched his for a moment longer, and then he turned, starting the engine.

Once more, the music soothed her. The movement of the car and the effects of wine relaxed her. It wasn't long before her eyelashes drifted shut. Yet, she wasn't quite asleep when she felt Howard covering her hand with his. And she smiled.

CHAPTER FOUR

Why did she startle at every phone call? Grace had no reason to think Howard would phone her. In fact, he had left her at her door Saturday night with a formal handshake, a curious grin, but not a word about seeing her again.

That was fine. Did she really want the complications of dating? At fifty-eight, she'd finally found freedom from responsibility. A bit of peace. As she'd told June Hobson, a man didn't fit into her idea of a new life.

Yet, every time the phone rang, Grace jumped. She would rush to the landline phone in the kitchen as if expecting Howard to be on the other end. It made her feel like a teenager. But the shortness of breath, the rush of excitement seemed silly at her age.

Once, after almost breaking her neck to reach the phone before it quit ringing, she was disappointed that it was merely her daughter Kelly. They were estranged, to say the least, but the wedding of Grace's granddaughter in late April was something safe for them to discuss.

"C.B. wants you to wear pale blue," Kelly informed Grace, in her most imperious way. "The mothers and grandmothers are wearing tea length. Do you need help picking out something suitable?"

"No, I don't." Grace was hardheaded enough not to be honest with her daughter. She'd already purchased "something suitable."

"Good. This is an elegant affair, Mother. Please don't disappoint."

"I have no intention of disappointing," Grace had replied and then silently hung up, ending their conversation as she'd ended so many others. It was difficult to talk to Kelly.

The truth was Colleen, or C.B. as Kelly called Grace's granddaughter, had already visited Heritage Springs earlier that month, chatting with Grace about the wedding, gushing about her fiancé Daniel, and asking her to wear pale blue. Bless, Colleen. The young woman gave Grace hope that the trouble with Kelly might be resolved one day.

Years ago, Kelly had made it clear she was angry with Grace, feeling hurt and betrayed. Granted, Grace's lack of support had caused hostility on Kelly's part. But no matter how many times Grace wished to make amends, she could never breach Kelly's stubbornness. So their rift remained—sad and painful.

After Colleen's visit, June had driven Grace to Lexington for a shopping spree. The dress Grace found was, of course, a shade of light blue and tea length, just as requested. It was the most beautiful garment Grace had ever put on her body—a princess cut chiffon dress with spaghetti-straps and a lace, long sleeve jacket. She felt elegant in it, almost like a different woman, the woman she longed to be.

But Howard Scott had thrown a monkey wrench in her carefully crafted widowhood. For the week after their date, Grace went about her business, telling herself it didn't matter if he didn't call.

They weren't in a relationship. He didn't have to call her. Besides, she wasn't going to give control of her life again to a man. And before she knew it, Thursday arrived and so did the afternoon grief support group.

When Howard came in, he sat across the circle, gazing at her, his features strong and unmistakably masculine. Grace watched him, hardly able to catch her breath. Despite her outward calm, her heart beat in erratic rhythm. What was the connection between them? Did she imagine it? She broke eye contact and looked away.

June began the session with a general question to the group. "How have you been this week?"

Nods and smiles greeted June. "It was great," one woman said.

The woman who had been in tears last week reported, "I survived."

"My week was very busy," Howard told the women in the circle. "Plus, I had a very nice dinner with friends on Saturday night."

Grace quickly glanced up at Howard and their gazes locked—his eyes a piercing blue. She ducked her head, suddenly bashful. Panic gnawed at her. Surely the whole group could see the heat in her cheeks.

"Grace, how about you?" June singled her out.

Grace gathered herself. How was she going to answer? She would never confess she'd spent the week hugging her phone waiting for Howard to call.

"My week was very uneventful." Leveling a pointed look at Howard, she smiled reluctantly. "It was quiet. Boring, in fact."

"Well, we can remedy that," June announced. "The church has asked us to help get ready for the July Fourth celebration in the square. Once again we're going to raise money for the Heritage

Springs Children's Club. I know you're a big supporter of that organization, Howard."

"Yes, it's a worthy cause."

"So you see," June went on. "Between now and July, none of us will have time to be bored."

Grace sensed June's motivation. If they were working, they wouldn't have time to be sad. Busyness was thought to be a therapy for grief.

~

AFTER A LONGER SESSION THAT DAY, Grace came out of the church to find daylight fading. The air had grown crisp, promising a spate of cold weather. Grace paused on the top steps and pulled on her leather gloves. The church door opened behind her, and Howard was suddenly by her side. He didn't say anything. He didn't ask permission, simply fell in beside her as she went down the front steps.

Was he walking her home again? His presumption both thrilled and unnerved her. Grace didn't know what to say to him so kept a steady pace up the hillside, her gaze straight ahead, her breath white against the waning light of the afternoon. When they stopped on her doorstep, the silence between them seemed way too awkward.

"Oh, heavens," she muttered, making up her mind. Tossing back her head, she met his eyes. "Would you like to come in? I have coffee and tea."

Or me?

Immediately, she blushed. Had she really thought that? Did he remember, just as she did, the sexy sixties book *Coffee, Tea or Me?*

She'd seen it on her father's bedside table when she was a kid and flipped through it before it suddenly disappeared after her mother caught her looking at it.

For goodness sakes, she wasn't offering herself. Would he think her remark presumptuous?

But he was grinning at her as if he remembered the book too. And as if he didn't mind her misstep, laughter crinkled his eyes. He seemed good-natured. Friendly. Uncritical.

"I'd love a cup of coffee," he said, "if you'll have one with me."

"I'd be honored."

Grace brought him into her home, trying not to wonder if he would compare it to his house in the Locust Grove subdivision, the better part of town. What did it matter? At her age, she couldn't worry about that. In fact, determined *not* to worry about appearances, she took him to the kitchen. She felt comfortable there. Less vulnerable. A framed cross-stitch picture hung on the wall that read *No matter where I serve my guests, it seems they like my kitchen best.* She'd hung the sampler soon after Lee's death in a display of independence since her husband had been critical of her hobby.

"Please have a seat," she said, and went about gathering the ingredients for the coffee maker.

"You have a lovely home."

Grace brought a small glass pitcher filled with half-and-half to the kitchen table. "Thank you. I've cleaned it out since my husband's death, gotten rid of a lot of junk, but there is so much more to get rid of. I really should downsize."

"It's hard, don't you think? After a spouse dies?"

"Yes, but no harder than when Lee was alive."

Howard had the kindness not to question her remark. Why had she said that about Lee? Not many people knew the truth about her husband—how hard he was to live with, how controlling. Kelly knew of course, but she'd had the good sense to leave long ago.

As she surveyed Howard Scott, smelling the woody spice of his aftershave, a wave of understanding washed over her, an insight that was the culmination of the year of soul searching. She caught her breath suddenly and turned away. Sticking with her husband had been Grace's choice and now she knew why.

Blood rushed to her head, making her dizzy. Why had she never thought of it that way?

Covering her confusion, she reached for the cabinet door and brought out her finest bone china—two teacups and saucers glazed in bright white and accented with platinum rims. She never used her wedding china, but this afternoon called for her best.

After pouring coffee and serving slices of banana bread on china plates, Grace sat down beside her guest. She added half-and-half to her coffee and brought the cup to her lips.

Howard sipped his coffee then placed his cup on the saucer. "Once again I fear I've said something to trouble you."

"No, no." He had read her reaction wrong. "It's just that something struck me just now. Something very profound. As if a light went on in my head."

He glanced briefly at her under his eyelashes and then picked up the coffee cup again. "Do you care to share it with me?"

Grace forced herself to breathe slowly. "I don't know."

"It might help if I told you I haven't been able to get you out of my mind all week."

"You haven't? I mean, really?"

"Yes, really, Grace."

"Oh, my goodness."

He looked soberly into her eyes. "So, you see, I have only your best interests at heart. If you need someone to confide in, I'll be happy to listen."

Something about this man charmed her. His formality. His decency. For some reason, there seemed to be a strange vibe between them, more than a physical connection, for sure.

Heavens don't go there. Sexual thoughts hadn't crossed her mind for ages.

Caught in the moment, Grace took a leap of faith. "Have you ever experienced an insight, so deep that it speaks to your very soul?"

His gaze questioned hers. "Go on."

"Just now, as we were talking, I understood why I stayed with my husband through all those years of unhappiness."

Howard didn't say anything. The compassion in his eyes and his attentiveness told her he cared.

"I stayed out of guilt. My guilt. I always knew that. We'd been indiscrete before we were married and got caught. I felt I must pay the consequences." Her explanation was evasive at best. She just couldn't bring herself to put the whole truth into words.

"This may sound odd to you, Howard, but I realize now I also stayed to punish him. By not divorcing him, I was a constant reminder of our carelessness. He couldn't escape it, and neither could I. By staying married all those years, never divorcing, we punished each other, don't you see?"

Howard took another sip of coffee as if to let her revelation sink in. "I'm not sure I totally understand, not knowing what you believe to be your carelessness."

"Yes, of course." What had made her think he'd comprehend?

He reached across the table and took her hand. "You don't need to tell me your history, Grace. We all make mistakes. That is how we learn. The fact my presence here helped you gain self-awareness is all that matters to me."

Why had she stupidly opened up to this man? It was as if their fledgling friendship had taken a serious turn. And it frightened her. But her sudden perception had been important to her. If telling him scared him away, what did she care? She had no intentions of anything coming from this friendship. She simply wanted to live a little.

And she felt pleasantly alive in his presence.

CHAPTER FIVE

Conversation turned from profound to silly, and by the time Howard left, darkness had fallen and Grace was laughing out loud. She hadn't laughed in a long time.

Watching him stride down the sidewalk, she noticed the street lamps captured his tall, athletic frame and strong set of his shoulders. Sure, his face was wrinkled and his hair gray, but the man still had much to give. There was a lot of living left in him. She hoped she could in some way be part of it.

Why was she yearning for his friendship? *Well, duh! Because I've never had such a relationship, stupid.* She'd kept herself isolated from people. Isolated from life. She *did* want to experience life. She wasn't dead yet!

Surprised by the direction of her thoughts, Grace turned away from the window and dropped the lace curtains. The darkness made it feel later than six o'clock.

After straightening the kitchen and eating a sandwich for supper, Grace went to bed with a good book. Books had been her friends for years, but tonight after reading for an hour, she couldn't get into the romance. She couldn't relate to the twenty-something heroine who threw herself in the path of the hunky hero. Taking off her reading glasses, she turned the book upside down on her chest and rubbed her eyes.

For the first time since Lee died, she hated being alone in bed. She focused on the footboard, staring at the spiraled bedposts, looking into the past. Yes, she had plenty of regrets, but at the time things happened, could she have done them differently? What if she'd been stronger, like Kelly? Could she have broken out of the mold she'd poured herself into all those years ago? Devoted mother. Dutiful wife. Grace had lost herself in the process of trying to be moral.

What a shame.

That was one idea of the young she liked—being true to yourself and getting past your hang-ups. She'd not been able to do it then. What about now? What was different? Was Howard the difference?

But who was she to presume? Hadn't wrong assumptions gotten her into trouble with Lee years ago?

He has sex with you so that means he loves you.

How naive had she been? Pretty innocent. Many girls in her day weren't as world-wise as today, especially small town girls with old-fashioned values. She'd made a misstep a long time ago and had paid for it ever since.

WHEN GRACE's bedside phone rang, she startled awake. Glancing at the clock, she discovered it was past ten. Not late, by any means. She'd fallen asleep with her thoughts, the book remaining open on her chest.

"I'm sorry to call you so late."

It was Howard. Why was he calling her?

"Is everything all right?"

"Wonderful! Perfect!" There was excitement in his voice. "Remember the talk of our syndicate horses?"

"Yes." Where was this leading?

"Our mare, Lady Success, foaled tonight."

"Oh, that's exciting."

"It's a colt. I was wondering if you'd like to come with me tomorrow to see him."

Is this a date? But she wasn't going to ask him. That seemed presumptuous. She shouldn't go. She had no idea why he was being so nice or what he wanted from her. She shouldn't let her imagination wander or give into the fantasy of her thoughts.

But wasn't she through with *shoulds*? Hadn't she told herself that? Wasn't it a perfect opportunity to do something about her promise to herself? Wasn't this "living a little?"

"I'd love to go with you, Howard," she said softly.

Woodson Stone Farm in central Kentucky was in the heart of the Bluegrass horse country and only twenty-five miles from Heritage Springs. The day was sunny and cold. Howard picked her up at ten. He was wearing brown corduroys and a tan wool sweater under his coat. She'd chosen her only pair of blue jeans, a turtleneck, and cardigan sweater. They were going to a barn, after all. It might be messy and certainly chilly.

Yet she felt underdressed in Howard's presence, even though he said, "You look lovely," when he helped her on with her coat.

They drove the winding roads to the farm in companionable silence past hillsides dotted with horses and old stone fences and white wooden ones, so typical of Kentucky. She sensed a kinship between them that seemed to grow every time they met.

Several miles into the trip, Howard asked, "How much do you know about Thoroughbreds?"

"I'm afraid I couldn't pass a test on them," Grace admitted. Lee, with his dull working-class life, had never gone to a racetrack, and always in his shadow, neither had she.

"Let me give you a quick lesson then," he said. "Thoroughbreds are bred between February and late May. They must be bred with a live cover meaning a stallion actually mounts the mare. No artificial insemination for these horses."

Howard took his gaze from the road and turned his head to smile at her, a confident, manly smile. As she grinned in return, Grace felt goose bumps rise along her arms, and she crossed them.

Looking back at the road, he continued, "Gestation is eleven months, but the universal birthday for all Thoroughbreds is January first. That's why we were lucky to have an early-March foal this season. When it's time for the three-year-old races leading to the Kentucky Derby, our foal will be one of the older horses."

"Because he was born closer to January first, it will make him more mature than ones born later in the spring."

"Exactly. You catch on quickly."

Grace felt the heat of a blush at the compliment. Expressions of praise had been few and far between when she was married.

Then out of the blue, Howard said, "I love how your cheeks redden."

Her face flamed hotter. Would she ever get used to this man and his flattery?

Several miles down the road, they turned into an open gate and drove between black board fencing until they reached a group of barns. After parking in front of one, Howard hopped out, rushed around the front of the vehicle, and opened the passenger-side door.

The bite of the winter's day struck Grace as she stepped onto the gravel. A man dressed in khaki jeans, a ski jacket, and a Woodson Stone Farm ball cap came out to greet them.

"Howard!" The two men shook hands.

"Grace, may I introduce Brownie Parsons? He's the broodmare manager at the farm."

"How do you do?" Grace accepted the man's bear-like hand. Brownie was perhaps in his late forties with a head of black hair and a ruddy complexion.

"Glad to meet you, ma'am. I knew Howard would be the first one out here to see the new foal."

"It's so near," Howard said, as if offering an explanation.

The manager turned to usher them into the barn. "No, sir, you are the only one with the passion for horse breeding. The others view it as purely an investment."

One more hint into the man who had crashed into the boundaries of her life, turning her world upside down. Grace smiled to herself, steeling herself against the odd thrill in her chest. What was happening to her? She'd best be on guard or she'd grow too dependent on Howie Scott.

The barn was a converted tobacco shed fitted with twenty square stalls large enough for foaling. Each one was bedded with straw that spilled from the stall doors into the aisle. The asphalt walkway was covered with interlocking rubber mats. As the trio strolled along the aisle, peering into each stall, their footfalls were muffled by the rubber.

"Here she is," Brownie announced at an end stall.

Lady Success was deep red, her coat shaggy and nicked from living outside. Beside her in the stall was a red colt with a long white blaze and striking white socks on his long, wobbly legs. He peeked at Grace and Howard from behind his mother, as if curious to see the newcomers.

Howard stuck a hand in his pocket and pulled out a round peppermint candy. He unwrapped the cellophane, and the mare's ears pricked forward. She hung her head over the stall door.

"I've spoiled her," Howard confided to Grace. He turned to Brownie. "May I?"

"She's your horse, sir."

Howard grinned like a school kid and put the peppermint in his palm. Making his hand flat, he offered the round candy. "Here you go, Lady."

The mare licked up the candy, crunching it between her teeth.

"The old girl has a sweet tooth," Howard said.

Brownie took what looked like a dog leash from a hook on the stall. "Let's give the little fellow a taste of Kentucky sunshine."

He entered the stall with caution. Lady moved away from the door to guard her colt. Satisfied Brownie was no threat, Lady accepted his presence. Then the manager fitted a halter over her head and threaded the leather line through it.

Howard took Grace's hand and pulled her aside. "We need to give them room."

Brownie led out the mare, her hooves making soft whop sounds on the rubber mats, and the hours-old colt followed behind, his short strides making it hard for him to catch up to his longer-limbed mother. Howard and Grace fell in behind the little procession.

Howard, however, observed other things. "He's got good confirmation in his hind end and through his legs."

"I guess that's a good thing."

"Damn important."

"All I want to do is give him a big hug," Grace admitted. "He's so fuzzy and adorable."

Howard chuckled and squeezed her hand. "You are so cute."

Grace didn't know about that. Breath caught in her throat, and she was unsure of a response.

None was needed, because the manager had reached the paddock with the mare. He led her through the gate and turned her loose. The colt hesitated outside. Lady swung her head back toward her foal and nickered softly. The baby scampered inside the paddock, puffs of steam coming out of his nose. Turning as the gate closed behind him, the colt watched the strange people. His mother, unconcerned about her human audience, dropped her head onto the dull late winter grass and began to graze.

"Best get back to work," Brownie said. "Stay as long as you like."

"Thank you for all you do," Howard said, offering the farm manager his hand.

The two men shook hands again. "My pleasure."

Grace watched the employer-employee exchange, impressed by the respect the two men had for each other. She'd never seen Lee interact with people like that. He'd been angry. Defensive. Disrespectful to a fault. She should have divorced him years ago, but she'd gotten stuck. That had been her mistake. But change had been impossible. Or so she had thought at the time.

Stepping up to the paddock fence, Grace touched its hard railing and gazed at the mare and foal. Howard joined her. He didn't know her thoughts. Her regrets. He accepted her as she presented herself, and she was overwhelmed by his acceptance.

"Look at him, Grace. This could be the one," Howard said, awe in his voice.

Surveying Howard's face, his eyes shining with hope, Grace smiled. "Yes, he could be the one," she said softly and wondered to herself if she was talking about Howard or the newborn foal.

CHAPTER SIX

But Howard couldn't be "the one." She'd vowed there would never be another one. What was she letting herself fall into? She'd slipped into marriage with Lee. It had not been intentional. It had simply happened when she'd gotten pregnant. Grace didn't want to live her life like that again. Without a sense of control. Without deliberately making a choice about what steps she'd take regarding her future.

The only way she knew how to handle her sudden jumble of feelings was to put distance between herself and Howard.

"You can't quit the support group," June said the next morning over tea. "You just joined."

"I'm going to." Grace stared into her cup as if reading the tea leaves.

"Why?"

She'd kept secrets in the past. Not telling June the truth was easy enough. "I'm going to be too busy."

June continued to press. "Doing what?"

"Ah—I'm going to get a job."

"A job?"

"Yes, for the money," she lied.

June let out a disgusted huff. "Howard Scott is a nice man." Her regard settled on Grace's face. "What are you afraid of?"

"I'm not afraid of anything."

"You can't fool me. Wasn't it only a few weeks ago you said you were tired of being scared? You said you wanted to get out more. Live a little."

"Well, now I need to get a job."

"I swear, Grace Baron, you are a contradiction."

Grace shrugged. "I guess that makes me human."

"Or foolish more like it."

So on Saturday morning, Grace walked to the town square looking for employment. She found a part-time job at the Country Affair Antiques Store, a small specialty shop. She'd never worked a day in her life, so taking the job was another leap of faith. Ironically, she wasn't willing to take another kind of leap—into the open arms of a man who acted as if he cared for her.

Avoiding Howard was not difficult. She didn't attend Sunday services. She didn't answer the phone. Without an answering machine, it rang and rang. Stopped. Then rang again. If he came by her house, she wasn't home. She was down at the square learning how to use a new-fangled credit card device.

Thursday afternoon came and went. Grace stayed home. Not scheduled to work, she puttered around her house. It was the cleanest the place had been in years. Clean and sterile. A tomb of her own making.

Late that afternoon when a vigorous knock almost crashed down her door, she knew it was Howard. A light burned in the living room so she had unwisely advertised she was home.

Okay, stop being afraid. Take your medicine.

Dropping the dust rag on an end table, Grace went to the door. He stood in the entrance, bigger than life, more handsome than she remembered.

"Why are you avoiding me?"

"I'm not."

"You are."

She swallowed her fear and stuck out her chin. "I don't know what you mean."

"Why have you left the group?"

"I'm working."

"That's a poor excuse."

How dare he doubt her? "Pardon me?"

Angry frustration showed in his eyes. He scrubbed a hand over his mouth, took a breath, and then asked, "May I come in?"

That was the last thing she wanted, but she couldn't very well keep him standing in the cold.

Silently, Grace stepped aside. Howard crossed the threshold into her living room. Immediately his presence ignited the room with energy, mirroring the vitality of the man that brought it.

"You owe me a better explanation."

"I owe you nothing."

"My God, Grace, have I done something to upset you?"

"Yes." She threw her shoulders back. "I mean no!"

For some reason, it was easy to stand up to this man. Why was she able to hold her ground? Defend her position? Because he wasn't Lee, and he didn't frighten her?

Breath hitched in her throat at the sudden realization. She wasn't really scared of Howard Scott, only of herself and her reaction to him.

He hesitated the span of several heartbeats, and she almost melted under his wounded expression.

"Please tell me what I've done, Grace."

"You haven't done anything, Howard," she said. "It's just—." Just what?

"Perhaps you aren't giving me enough credit."

Grace surveyed him silently, heart pounding against her ribs.

"Talk to me, Grace," he pleaded again. "Do you know how crazy I was all week when I couldn't get in touch with you? I thought something was wrong. You were sick. Then I realized it must have been something I'd done."

She wanted to crumble before his eyes. Back down from her stance. But she'd promised herself to control her life. Slipping into an easy friendship with this man had made her head spin. Where was the power in that? Certainly not with her.

"You've always been a gentleman," she said through dry lips. "I could not have asked for a better experience with you. I've enjoyed dinner. Seeing the horses."

"I thought I was taking it slow, respecting your reticence. I'm sorry if I overstepped."

Looking away, Grace fought the regret rising in her throat. If she wasn't afraid of Howard, who was she afraid of? Of losing control again. Of falling too quickly for a man she didn't know. Of making another mistake.

She turned back her gaze to connect with his. Once again the power of their bond overwhelmed her. "It isn't you, Howard." Longing to grasp his hand, she clasped hers behind her back.

"Then what is it, Grace?" Howard wasn't as reserved. He reached out and seized her hand in his two big ones. He drew it up to his lips, drawing her nearer to him, and kissed the back of her hand as if he were a gentleman in a movie.

"I'm so unsure of myself," Grace whispered, watching his lips linger on her hand.

"Do I frighten you?"

"No!" He didn't. "I scare myself."

His shoulders relaxed. His expression softened. "Good. It's not me then." He glanced around the room. "May we sit down?"

Without her answer, he pulled her toward the sofa. They sat down together, shoulder to shoulder. They didn't speak. Somewhere in the house, a clock ticked loud enough to be heard in the silence.

Finally, Grace dragged forth the question on her mind. "I don't know what you want from me, Howard."

He took up her hand again and ran his fingers across her palm. "I want to get to know you."

"But why?"

"Because I like you."

"Why?"

He grinned at her. "Twenty questions?"

"No, I want to understand. Why me? Why now?"

"How can a person explain why he likes someone? I don't know, Grace." He seemed disconcerted. His eyes grew perplexed. "I simply feel an attraction to you. As if we are meant to be with each other."

She felt it too, this connection. But she couldn't admit it to him. To herself? No. That was even more dangerous.

"Don't you see? That's the problem," Grace said. "You want to remarry. I don't."

He nodded. "I thought that might be the problem."

"So I can't continue to see you, no matter how pleasant our times together have been. It wouldn't be fair to you."

"How about you letting me decide that?" His gaze landed on her face. "I can be the judge of what is fair to me."

"I don't want to lead you on. I don't want to raise your expectations."

"Fair enough. What if I tell you that even knowing the conditions going in, I still want to be with you?"

Grace frowned and shook her head. "I'd say you're crazy."

"My son has already told me that." Howard laughed at himself.

That seemed to settle it. Howard was crazy, and she'd be crazy too if she continued to see him. Yet a huge part of her heart urged her on. She wanted to live a little, didn't she? There wasn't much chance of that happening if she turned Howard Scott away. Not many men in Heritage Springs were beating down her door to meet her.

"What if I agreed to see you?"

"Would you?"

"Under the stipulation that you realize I have no intention of going to bed with you or, for that matter, doing something as stupid as marrying you."

He laughed aloud. "Oh, Grace, you are so lovable! I appreciate your honesty."

Honesty? She'd been anything but that. However, it felt good for the first time to express herself, to communicate in a way so that Howard knew exactly where she stood. And she felt suddenly free to be with him without worry. No expectations. Just a good time.

She was free to live a little.

CHAPTER SEVEN

For the rest of March, Howard courted Grace, much like his dad told him he'd dated his mom after World War II. He liked the sound of the old-fashioned word, wondering if he'd ever courted his other two wives like this. Probably not, but Grace needed special attention. From what June told him, Grace's life with her husband had been hard and her daughter's voluntary exile even harder. He was not above showering Grace with a little TLC.

On Saturday, after her shift ended at the antiques store, Howard picked her up at her house and whisked her to a winery for dinner. Located near Lexington, the small venue was surrounded by rows of dormant grape vines. It had a bottling facility that they skipped seeing and a cozy, gourmet restaurant with a warm blaze in the stone fireplace.

"Have you ever been here?" he asked, lifting his glass of wine to her.

Grace blushed in that delicious way he liked. "No," she replied with a delighted look in her eyes. She returned his salute with her wine goblet.

The next weekend he drove her to Louisville to attend a Broadway Series play in the Kentucky Center for the Arts. On a Saturday when she didn't work, Howard booked a private bourbon distillery tour. They saw three different distilleries, sampled their various wares, and dined in Lexington that evening. Grace returned home quite giddy, claiming she'd never, ever had a better day.

He wanted it that way. He wanted her smiling and happy. Making her happy pleased him. In fact, he was content again for the first time since his second wife's death.

That's when he realized he wanted a future with Grace Baron.

What she wanted was another matter, of course.

Grace had surprised herself by liking her new job. Clerking at the Country Affair Antiques Store was fun. She enjoyed helping others find the perfect treasure and was intrigued by the history of the consignment items people brought into the store to sell.

Often her work got in the way of Howard's plans for their outings. But that was fine. She didn't need to be free whenever he called. Years ago, her mother had cautioned her about being too available to boys, but of course, she hadn't listened. The rest, as they said, was history.

She liked toying with Howard too. Not in a mean way, but playing "hard to get" was turning into a joyful pastime. Of course, she had no intention of being "got." She'd told him that. He acted as if he understood, but he was certainly persistent. And he'd taken her to places she'd never been.

One Monday, the first week of April, Grace's shift was near its end when Howard walked into the store. Outside, storm clouds hung low and rain threatened.

"Howard!"

He smiled that manly smile that devastated her. She drew in a breath and offered a brief, nervous grin. She couldn't help responding to him. For some reason, his mere presence caused goose bumps to rise up on her arms.

Standing on the other side of the counter, he suddenly turned serious. "I came to drive you to my house," he said.

Grace had never been to his house and was not about to go now, especially when his tone had turned so insistent. "Whatever for?"

"Because there's a tornado watch, and I have a basement."

"Excuse me?"

"You'll be safer at my house if something should happen."

"I'm not going to your house."

Her words elicited a brief laugh. "Dammit, Grace Baron, why are you so stubborn?"

"And why are you such a control freak?"

"Because I care for you, that's why."

That brought her up short, and she stared at him a moment. Her heart hammered in her ears like the rumble of thunder in the distance.

"I'm going home."

"Okay, then I'll drive you."

"Suit yourself." She turned away from him and picked up her purse from beneath the counter. "Sally, I'm heading home," she called to the owner, who came out of the back storeroom.

"Be careful," Sally called.

Grace looked over her shoulder as she headed for the door. "Don't worry about me. Howard is driving me home."

She felt odd—in control, but vulnerable at the same time. She didn't feel beat down, filled with despair, as she had when married. No, she felt accepted for herself. Totally cared for and loved.

Her steps faltered.

She caught her breath.

Howard took her arm and ushered her out as the rain started to fall. He opened the car door, and she slid inside.

When he climbed into the driver's seat, Howard shot her a look mixed with concern and irritation. "I wish you'd let me take you to my house. This storm might be a bad one."

"I've ridden out plenty of bad storms in my house."

Silence filled the car. Was he mad? Grace glanced at Howard's set face, his eyebrows furrowed. He started the car. The ride home wasn't long. He pulled alongside the curb in front of her house and turned off the ignition.

Then he broke his silence. "I'm staying with you until this is over."

Grace opened her mouth to object.

"Dammit, Grace, this is the anniversary of the April 3rd, 1974, tornadoes."

Her eyes widened. She remembered that horrible, fear-filled day when Kentucky, Ohio, and much of the Midwest were over-whelmed by a record number of tornadoes. Louisville had been hit, but not as hard as Brandenburg, Kentucky. There had been more deaths in that small town than in Louisville. She'd been in high school then here in Central Kentucky and remembered the warm air sticky with humidity.

"I was in Louisville that day," Howard said, his face grim. "In law school at the university. I heard a roar of trains south of campus. That's where the tornado hit, a little more than a mile away from me, striking Freedom Hall and leveling the horse barns at the Fairgrounds."

"Oh, Howard." She brought her hand to her lips, understanding his concern.

"I've had a healthy respect for bad weather ever since."

She reached across the seat and squeezed his arm. "Okay. I appreciate your company."

They made a run for it, getting totally drenched before reaching the porch. Dripping water into a puddle on her hardwood floor, Howard looked like a drowned rat. Grace was no better herself, but she laughed at the once picture-perfect, manicured Mr. Scott with his wet hair plastered to his forehead. She hurried around the living room switching on lamps while Howard watched her. When finished, when the room was brighter, a contrast to the dark storm outside, Grace walked back to him.

"You can't stay in those wet clothes," she said in her best motherly tone.

His eyebrows lifted. "I'm beginning to like the way you think."

"Dream on!" Grace turned toward her bedroom. What did she have large enough for Howard to wear? She'd given Lee's clothing to charity, but he'd been a smaller man. Returning moments later with a bath towel and an extra large University of Kentucky sweatshirt, she offered them to him. "Maybe these will do."

Howard accepted the items, staring down at her for many long beats. Heart pounding against her ribs, Grace was caught in the moment. Would things become intimate? Did she want them to?

He took one step. Then thunder shook the house, rattling the windows.

"That was mighty damn close." Howard smiled as if to reassure her. "Point me toward your bathroom."

"Upstairs, first door on the left."

As he climbed the steps, Grace didn't know what to think. What to wish for? Her words said one thing. *No way, no how.* But her heart was beginning to yearn for another outcome.

"I'll turn on the television weather," she called after him. With the local weatherman blaring across the living room warning viewers of the storm, Grace hurried to her own bedroom downstairs, stripped off her wet clothing and dressed in sweat pants and shirt.

She was seated on the worn flowered sofa when Howard returned. He joined her, and they sat shoulder to shoulder. He'd not removed his khaki pants, but his feet were bare, and he wore the tight-fitting sweatshirt.

"A tornado warning was issued for Southern Indiana," Grace told him.

"Hopefully, it won't come toward the southeast."

They sat quietly a few minutes, staring at the flashing TV screen, each wrapped in their own thoughts. Grace felt the heat emanating from this big man. She felt his goodness and caring. She felt her own confusion—her agony of indecision mixed with a determination to do differently, be differently.

Another gigantic clap of thunder vibrated the room. Howard draped his arm over her shoulder.

"I think I should offer you some coffee. Or tea," she said to break the awkwardness of the moment.

"Or me," he whispered.

Another roar of thunder. Another flash of lightening. Then the lights flickered and the house went dark.

They sat for several seconds in the darkness, absorbed in the storm battering the house. Grace's nerves were on edge. Her heart raced. But it was more from Howard's presence than the thunderstorm.

"Oh, dammit, Grace."

She turned her eyes from the blackened TV screen to his, shadowed in the darkness. Were her upturned lips inviting? Did she mean for them to be?

"Oh, dammit, Grace," he said again. Then he pulled her into his arms and kissed her.

As she returned his kiss with equal fervor, she realized this was where she was meant to be. For the first time in her life, Grace felt she'd come home.

CHAPTER EIGHT

Colleen's rehearsal dinner was the following Friday evening in Louisville. Because Grace didn't have a car, Howard drove her to the downtown hotel and dropped her off. Grace didn't want him there even though he'd offered to escort her. She didn't want her daughter to know about him, because she didn't want anything ugly to spoil their fledgling relationship.

Besides she wasn't sure of it herself. A few passionate kisses, good vibrations, and fun times—what did they amount to in the long run? She didn't know if he wanted to marry her, even though his stated objective in group therapy was to marry again. But even though he'd been persistent in dating her, was she really his choice?

And what about her intention not to remarry? How could she lose herself again in another devastating relationship? So she thanked Howard for the ride and agreed to let him pick her up on Sunday. But share in a family event? *No.* Not when he was not family.

Bless Colleen. She stopped by Grace's hotel room before the evening rehearsal and dinner. It would take place in one of the hotel's event rooms. Kelly had chosen to ignore her mother during the festivities as if she only included her because of Colleen's wishes. Grace had understood her daughter's message all too well. Things were not right between them. Perhaps they never would be.

"Gran," Colleen said, hugging her grandmother, "I wanted to see if you have all that you need."

Grace returned the hug, holding her granddaughter a little longer than necessary, determined to be happy on this happy occasion. Unlike her mother, Colleen was blond. She had two cute dimples when she smiled and a pert little nose that was more pixie-like than Kelly's. She'd always been a happy child, a little naïve as Grace had been, and kind. In the age of social media, she often communicated with her intentionally backwards grandmother over the telephone and by impromptu visits to Heritage Springs.

"I'm so happy and excited for you," Grace said. "You and Daniel will have a beautiful life together."

Colleen flushed with happiness. "Yes, we will! Daniel is so perfect, Gran. I love him so much."

"I can tell that," Grace responded with a grin. "And your wedding will be just wonderful."

When she showed Colleen her grandmother-of-the-bride dress, her granddaughter exclaimed, "Oh, this is lovely! You may upstage the bride!"

"Pooh," Grace scoffed. "No one can upstage my beautiful granddaughter."

And so it went, chatting back and forth, until Colleen changed the subject abruptly. "I'm sorry about my mother," she said. "Daniel says she is an unhappy woman, and I shouldn't let her unhappiness cloud our marriage."

Grace sighed. "Daniel is right. I'm afraid your mother carries some heavy burdens."

"I don't understand her," Colleen complained, a frown marring her face. "And she's always mean to you."

"Your mother and I disagreed a long time ago."

"I know. That's when she moved to Louisville."

"Yes," Grace said with a nod. "Her father was very hard on her."

"Well, I'm not going to worry about ancient history. What about you, Gran? How are you doing?"

Yes, how was she doing? She'd come to suspect she was in love with Howard Scott. But she didn't want that, not if he didn't want it too. And was it right, at her age, after failing so miserably in her first marriage, to try again? What if she failed again? What if she ruined Howard's life as Lee said she'd ruined his?

Grace felt heat in her face. "I'm seeing a gentleman at home," she revealed with a sheepish grin.

Colleen clapped her hands together. "Oh, Gran! How lovely!"

"Yes, it has been," she said wistfully. "But I'm not sure how serious he is, or even if I want him to be serious."

"Of course you want him to be serious," Colleen countered. "You're not old. You deserve happiness just like everyone else."

"I know. But I thought I could make that happiness by myself. By doing my 'thing.' I haven't told you, I have a part-time job now," she said, changing the subject to avoid delving too deeply into her relationship with Howard.

"That's wonderful. But what's wrong with having a man complete you?"

"Are men supposed to do that? Your grandfather never did that for me. I lost myself somewhere along the way."

"Oh, you know what I mean." Colleen frowned as if trying to capture her thoughts into words. "A man should bring out the best in you. Allow you to be yourself. You should complement each other."

"Is that what Daniel does for you?"

Colleen flushed prettily. "Yes. We're a great team. Oh, I'm so happy, Gran!"

"I know, sweetheart. You look happy. I'm happy for you."

Pausing a beat, Colleen cast a serious gaze toward her. "Don't be afraid to love again, Gran. If not this gentleman friend, maybe you'll find someone else. But never be afraid to love. It's never too late to find true love."

Grace took a step back. "Funny. That's what Howard says too."

THE WEDDING OVER, life returned to the new normal for Grace—work, support group, morning tea with June and, of course, visits with Howard. He'd taken her to a Reds baseball game at Great American Ball Park in Cincinnati, and they'd watched an afternoon of races at the Keeneland Racecourse in Lexington. Her world had expanded because of Howard, and she'd learned she enjoyed going out and doing. All those years of being a homebody seemed so wasted and sad. Tonight she'd finally had the nerve to cook for him.

He reached across the kitchen table and touched her hand. "I want to marry you, Grace. You know that, don't you?"

Uncomfortable, Grace stood and went to the stove. "Would you care for more spaghetti or another slice of bread?"

"I'm serious," was all he said.

Grace turned to look at him. He was watching her through half-hooded eyes. He was so handsome. Such a gentleman. He'd not made a move other than to kiss her. And, oh, how Howie could kiss! She treasured his ability to keep his promise. No going to bed, she'd told him. And he'd wined and dined her, treated her like a queen, just as she'd longed to be treated in her daydreaming days as a teenager, but never put pressure on her to have sex, unlike Lee who had manipulated her into the back seat of his '73 Chevy on their third date.

Now that it was out in the open—this obstacle between them—she didn't know what to say. Part of her thrilled at his words. At his honorable intentions. Part of her longed to be swept away, protected and cherished for the rest of her life. But could she accept his proposal? The other part of her said she wasn't ready. It had to be in her own time. Of her own making.

"You know I love you," he said quietly.

Her stomach in knots, she dropped her gaze to focus on her feet. Her heart yearned to say yes, but the stubborn part of her being held her back.

"I'm not ready yet," she said in a tiny voice. She lifted her gaze. "I'm sorry, Howard."

A spasm of regret twisted her heart when she saw his face. It would be so easy to agree to his proposal. It would be so easy to let him wine and dine her forever. But at what cost? Herself?

"You'll not be rid of me easily," Howard predicted.

"I don't want to be rid of you." She clasped her hands together in fear.

He grinned that heart-stopping grin and sat back. "Don't worry, dear. I'm not going anywhere."

CHAPTER NINE

Always true to his promises, Howard continued to call and come by. He even made plans to take her to the Kentucky Derby the first Saturday in May. She'd lived in Kentucky all her life but had never been to the Derby.

With the event only a few weeks away, choosing something to wear at such short notice soon became a problem. June drove her to a mall in Lexington. At Macy's they found a black suit with an A-line skirt that hit Grace's knees, and they paired it with a white blouse. She could remove the jacket if it became hot, but the first Saturday in May always had unpredictable weather. A jacket might feel good. Then they searched for a hat, something to go with the suit, and found a black satin and feather fascinator with a fishnet mesh veil.

"My mother wore a veil like this in the 'fifties," Grace said. "I remember it as a kid."

"Strange how fashions come and go," June remarked.

"What goes around, comes around," Grace acknowledged with a grin.

The important dilemma solved, Grace was free to anticipate the very long Derby day to come.

~

"I've never seen so many people except on television." Grace stared at the racetrack infield with its general admission revelers already partying at noon. Over one hundred and sixty thousand people attended each Kentucky Derby, in the infield, in the grandstands, and in the fancy, air-conditioned seating areas for the rich and famous.

"Quite the tradition," Howard said. "Like pretty girls and hats."

He meant her, and she accepted his compliment without her normal blush. Was she getting used to having Howard Scott around?

They shared an expensive box seat—six folding chairs in the reserved section near the finish line—with two of his syndicate partners, Mr. and Mrs. Drake and Bob and Margeaux Smithson. Of course, Margeaux outshone Grace, wearing a skimpy, flowered sundress and a huge flowered hat. Under the bright May sunshine, her complexion looked taut in just the right places, but she couldn't hide the wrinkles in her neck or the age spots on the backs of her hands.

Okay, she was being spiteful, Grace had to admit, but the woman rubbed her the wrong way, not in the least because she guessed Margeaux's ultimate goal was Howard.

And Howard's my man.

Where had that come from?

But she didn't have time to dwell on the annoying Margeaux Smithson. There was a full afternoon of undercard races, many of them graded stakes races which Howard explained were the highest level of all. His horse, the syndicate's Thoroughbred, wouldn't run until the race right after the Kentucky Derby. It was an optional claiming race, going seven furlongs on the dirt. As Howard told her, a claiming race was one in which a horse could be bought by anyone for the specified "claiming" price. Although his horse was not at the level of better stakes horses running that day, the syndicate chose not to run the three-year-old as a "claimer," because the horse had potential.

The group wiled away the afternoon picking horses, placing bets, and drinking traditional mint juleps, an iced drink consisting of bourbon, mint, and sugar syrup. Well, to put it more bluntly, Margeaux enjoyed several mint juleps whereas Grace could only stomach one simply to say she'd sipped it at the Derby.

At one point in the afternoon, Grace was left in the box sitting beside Bob Smithson. Everyone else was away standing in lines for the bathrooms or placing bets.

The older gentleman cleared his throat causing Grace to glance up from her racing program.

"I must say, Mrs. Baron, you seem to have blossomed since I last saw you. February was it?"

"Yes, I came to dinner at your house in February."

"And Howard looks happy."

Now Grace blushed. She felt the heat creep up her cheeks. "I'm glad."

The man returned to studying his program. The conversation ended. But the implications of Bob's remarks spun around in Grace's head. Had she blossomed? Was she different for knowing Howard?

He returned at that moment carrying a huge waffle cone full of vanilla and chocolate soft serve ice cream. "For you, my dear," he said and presented it to her with a tiny, formal bow.

She giggled. "Just what I've been longing for."

"Eat up fast. It's beginning to drip."

As Grace licked the ice cream, catching the drips with her tongue, she wondered at Howard once more. Lee would never have acknowledged her sweet tooth with a cone of ice cream.

But Howard had swept into her world, turning it upside down and showing her a side of life she'd never experienced. So much was different. Now she could enjoy a simple gift and a sincere compliment. She'd taken a leap of faith and gotten a part-time job. She'd opened up about her feelings—well some of them anyway—in the grief support group. She and June were best friends again since their high school days. And because of Howard, she'd done and seen things she'd never thought to see and do.

Yes, since February she'd changed so much.

And she liked that change. In fact, her life was close to being perfect. Her relationship with her daughter still troubled her, but maybe she could remedy that some day. And she was tired of thinking about Lee, of comparing Howard to Lee. She was wasting her time dwelling on the past. The old heartaches. The mistakes. Now it was time to be young again, lighthearted, and looking forward to her future.

Grace glanced at Howard beside her, a solid presence in her life. She didn't want to lose him. But she didn't want to lose herself again either.

As she finished the last crunch of the messy cone, Grace felt the truth seep through her slowly. She was a different person now than when she'd been married to Lee. She'd created that new person, but Howard—no, Howie—had helped. Bottom line—Howie Scott made her better. When she was with him, she didn't lose herself at all.

Grace watched all the preliminaries on the Jumbotron. The huge television screen in the infield showed the Derby horses in the paddock. The jockeys arrived and mounted. Soon the bugler dressed in red came out of the pagoda in the winner's circle and played the call to the post. As the first Thoroughbred stepped onto the track and the twenty-horse field paraded in front of the grandstands, the University of Louisville Marching Band played Stephen Foster's "My Old Kentucky Home."

"I love the tradition," Howard said above the roar of the crowd.

Grace looked up at him. *And I love you.* Her heart warmed at the thought, and she smiled.

Soon "The Run for the Roses" was over and the winner was draped with the blanket of red roses in the winner's circle and crowded by owners and media. The first leg of the American Triple Crown was in the books.

But now Howard was tense, anticipating the next race. As the three couples picked their way through the departing crowd, Howard grabbed her hand to keep her close. At the entrance to the paddock, they showed their owners' badges and were allowed entry. In the grassy area inside the walking circle, they waited. Only an hour earlier, the Derby owners had awaited their horses here. Now Howard and his syndicate shared the same dreams as those racehorse owners.

Grace hoped all would turn out well for Howie…and for her. But she wasn't thinking about the upcoming race. She'd made up her mind.

❧

Howard fought the excitement building inside. It was the same way with each race—the anticipation of a win, the fear his horse would not come out of the race in good shape. The racing business was a crapshoot, but so was life. He savored the good times, and he endured the bad.

The syndicate's horse was a bay colt called Dallas in the barn, not his registered name. The horse was not good enough for the ranks of stakes runners, but he was bred well and sound. Dallas seemed to have a will to win. Having a horse with a heart was what every owner wanted.

At the call to the post, the horses left the paddock and walked down the passageway toward the track. Howard captured Grace's hand and tugged her along after him through the walkway to where they would watch the race from the owner's section next to the track. He was happy to share this experience with Grace. She took in everything like a kid with a new toy. Seeing life through Grace's eyes gave him a new appreciation for things he'd so often took for granted.

And she was a wise woman. She didn't pester him with questions as Margeaux pestered Bob. That type of behavior would drive him nuts, one of the many things he had disliked about his second wife.

The syndicate horse broke sharply and was comfortable setting off the pace in second place behind the leader. The two circled the track in that order until turning for home in the stretch. Dallas poked his head in front, and Howard joined the crowd cheering.

Grace jumped up and down, pumping Howard's arm. "Go, Dallas, go!"

None of his other wives had enjoyed his hobby with this kind of passion.

Through the last few furlongs, Dallas and the former leader were side-by-side, battling, each striving to win. When they charged under the finish line, Dallas was in front, prevailing by a half-length in a spectacular race.

Howard's heart soared. Excitement pumped through his body. "We won!" he shouted.

"We won! We won!" Grace bounced up and down beside him. "Oh, Howie! We won!"

She flung her arms around his neck, jumping against him with her own excitement. She felt so good. So right. As if she belonged there in his arms.

He couldn't help himself. He couldn't resist. Imprisoning her lips with his, he kissed her, as she deserved to be kissed—as he'd always wanted to kiss her.

"Oh, Howie," she murmured against his mouth.

He loved her new name for him. Did she realize what this meant? She'd emerged from the stiff formality of the past. She'd let herself go. She'd become her own person.

"Oh, Howie," she said again. "I want to marry you."

"What?" Had he heard her correctly? Gently pushing her away, Howard implored her with his eyes. "Don't say that unless you mean it."

She gazed up at him, a telltale blush staining her cheeks. "With all my heart."

"Oh, Grace," he said with a sigh.

"Will you marry me?" she asked again.

He laughed at himself. "This is a first. I've never been proposed to, but of course I'll marry you, darling Grace." He pulled her once more into his arms and held her tight. "And we'll make all our dreams come true and live happily ever after."

The End

I hope you enjoyed Howie and Grace's story. Please consider sharing your experience with your fellow readers by leaving a review.

II

SECRETS: BLUEGRASS HOMECOMING

Schoolteacher Kelly Baron raised her child alone. Now that her daughter's grown and married, Kelly can finally start her new life in North Carolina, responsible only for herself. She has just one more thing to do: help her mother. To do so, she must return to Heritage Springs, Kentucky, the place she'd fled years before. Back then she'd been nothing but a small-town girl from the wrong side of the tracks, hiding a secret that could have destroyed lives.

Newly divorced lawyer Rob Scott seeks solace for his heartache in his small-town roots. Maybe being an incurable romantic isn't smart for a lawyer who has to deal with hard facts. The last thing he's looking for is a relationship. He'd made millions in Chicago, but in his heart he's always kept a secret dream, a desire he's never told anyone. Then he runs into Kelly, the girl who'd disappeared from his life years ago, leaving behind only hurt and unanswered questions.

Kelly's kept her secret all these years. But sometimes the only way to build a future is to face the past.

CHAPTER ONE

Seneca Park
Louisville, Kentucky

"Kelly, will you marry me?"

Heat swept Kelly Baron's face, and it had nothing to do with the warm June day. Choking back dismay, she stared at the kneeling man at her feet. "For goodness sakes, Thomas, stand up."

Thomas struggled to his feet and sat down beside her on the park bench. His normally flushed face was peppered with sweat, and he had an expectant look in his eyes. "I'm serious," he said, fumbling in his pocket and withdrawing a small, black, velvet box. "Dead serious." He lifted the lid.

Secured inside the box was a spectacular princess-cut diamond solitaire set in a white gold, cathedral setting. Kelly was somewhat of an expert about diamond engagement rings because of her daughter's recent wedding, but she never expected Thomas Dunlap to offer her one, let alone one that looked to be the size of a carat.

Kelly focused on the beautiful ring, avoiding the conflicting emotions whirling in her head and the warning bells ringing in her ears.

Her usually reticent suitor became assertive and removed the ring from its box. "Here. Try it on."

Before Kelly could demur, Thomas grabbed her left hand and slipped the ring on the third finger.

"It's too big," were the only words she could force from her dry lips.

"That's no problem," Thomas said, bending over her hand. She could see the thinning spot of hair at the top of his head. He slid the ring up and down on her finger and then raised his eyes. "We can get it sized to fit. What do you think?"

"It's lovely."

"No, about marrying me."

That again. Panic set in. It's not that Kelly didn't like Thomas. They had been dating since his divorce. He was an elementary school principal in Jefferson County, and she taught fifth grade in a local Catholic school. They liked to walk for exercise, go to Broadway Series plays, and eat Italian. They had a lot in common. But she had never, ever considered marrying anybody, not even when she'd been pregnant with C.B. and needed to get married in the worst way.

"I'm not sure it's the right time," Kelly mumbled, looking at the way a thin strand of salt and pepper hair fell across his forehead.

Thomas sat back, opening a little space between them but continuing to hold her hand.

"It's a perfect time." His voice lowered turning persuasive. "We've dated five years. Colleen is happily married, and you finally settled your great-aunt's estate."

"But her house hasn't sold." She looked down, avoiding his gaze. Aunt Bess had left her house to both Kelly and Colleen, and when it sold her daughter and new husband would have a tidy nest egg.

"A technicality." Thomas grasped both hands and renewed his efforts. "Look, Kelly, you're not responsible for anyone but yourself now. It's time for you to do what you want and move forward with your life."

Kelly lifted her eyes to gaze into his face. She blinked. For twenty-one years she'd packed her life full of busyness and responsibility, spending her time taking care of first her daughter and later Aunt Bess. Thomas was right. All that responsibility was over. She would be forty in July. It was time to be a little selfish.

But did that include marrying Thomas?

She shook her head once. "I don't know. This is so——" her voice faltered, "—unexpected."

"I know it is, Kelly, darling. But you must have guessed how I feel about you."

Kelly dropped her gaze again, uncomfortable with his earnest, direct stare. Yes, she had known Thomas cared, but part of her had believed he would never marry again given the hideous nature of his divorce. It wasn't as if theirs was a platonic relationship. They enjoyed good enough sex twice a month, usually the weeks he didn't have his son.

She met his gaze again. "What about Clayton?"

"Clayton goes to college in the fall," he said. "Kelly, you and I are footloose and fancy free, sweetheart!" A smile transformed his face, smoothing out the worry lines in his brow, but leaving Kelly's chest tight. "We're good together, professionally and personally. It's now or never, darling."

Time for a forced smile. Did she want to spend the rest of her life with Thomas Dunlap? Become Mrs. Thomas Dunlap? No. For one thing, if she ever married, she would keep her maiden name. She would never succumb to an out-of-date tradition. And besides, she was too self-reliant, too used to doing what she pleased with only her daughter and her aunt to consider putting her life in the hands of another.

But Aunt Bess was dead and C.B. was married. Thomas was right. She *was* free.

"This is such a surprise. Will you let me think about it?" She hated the timid note that crept into her voice. Slowly, Kelly disengaged her hands and withdrew the sparkling ring from her finger. It was too much bling. It was too much pressure. She handed it back to him. "You know I don't do change well."

Thomas slid the ring back into its protective velvet box. He had the look of a man receiving a death sentence. *I hate to hurt his feelings.* She hadn't quite told him "no," but she hadn't said "yes." If the situation were reversed, she'd feel like shit.

"You have a habit of avoiding things," he said with a sharp shake of his finger, reprimanding her as if she was a six-year-old caught hitting another child on the playground. "It's a character flaw you need to work on."

Kelly shifted on the park bench. Thomas was always too blunt. That was *his* character flaw. She pressed her right hand hard against the bench and fought down her annoyance.

Yet could Thomas be right?

Twenty-one years ago she had avoided telling C.B.'s father she was pregnant, but that was because his mother had found out they were secretly dating and warned her away from him. She made it perfectly clear her son had a future that didn't include a small town girl from the wrong side of the tracks. It was evident she went behind her son's back because he never said anything about his mother's interference. Probably her husband didn't even know about her scare tactics.

But his mother was right. When they talked about life after high school, he made it clear he didn't intend to end up in a small town like his father. He intended to go places, be important. Kelly was never part of that future he painted for himself.

When she found out she was pregnant, Kelly couldn't tell him. He didn't love her. He would reject her and their child.

And so once Kelly started keeping the secret, she had never revealed the truth to anyone, especially not her own father, who had threatened to beat it out of her and confront the boy and his parents. It was just as easy to avoid telling her mother, who could be bullied by her husband, and later C.B., who accepted life without a father. Leaving her hometown and moving to Louisville put distance between her and the problem.

Thomas cleared his throat. "I won't wait forever," he told her.

"Of course not." Kelly shook off the memories and touched his sleeve. How did she soften her response? "I just need time to process this. Please?"

He kissed her then—a typical Thomas kiss with lips pressed firmly shut and eyes closed. Kelly responded as always, timidly, tepidly—trying to deny the longing in her heart for the love of her life, someone who cherished her, didn't want to change her and loved her just the way she was.

Someone she was too afraid to find.

"DID THOMAS REALLY SAY THAT?"

Ear pressed to her iPhone, Kelly nodded even though her best friend Rachel couldn't see the action. "Yes. You know how he is," she said.

Kelly leaned back against the headboard of her queen-sized bed with its cozy, apple green comforter and cotton sheets—her refuge from the untidy world where she lived. She'd never had sex in it. Thomas preferred the six hundred-thread count, extra deep Egyptian cotton sheets of his king-sized bed. What's more, he didn't like anyone touching him when he slept. She was used to sleeping alone, so part of her didn't mind.

Another part longed to be held all night long, tenderly cuddled and caressed, not taken for granted once the deed was done.

It was dark outside, almost ten o'clock. One lamp illuminated Kelly's cream-colored bedroom walls, casting shadows over her nightstand where her stack of to-be-read books was piled.

"What are you going to do?" Rachel's voice, low and soft, was not able to mask its cautionary note.

"About Thomas?" Kelly paused. "I don't think I'm the marrying kind."

She heard Rachel's sigh of relief almost as if her friend were in the same room, not seven hundred miles away. Did Rachel agree? When they met, Rachel was single and didn't have a child, but she'd always been willing to let C.B. tag along with them when they went out to eat or shop at the mall. Then Rachel met Carl on eDate.com and the rest, as they say, was history.

Rachel had taken the chance Kelly had never been willing to take. She had married Carl and moved away settling in Beaufort, North Carolina, where she and Carl ran a thriving bed and breakfast.

"Thomas is right about one thing." Rachel took a big breath as if gathering courage. "Your life is wide open. It's time for you to start fresh."

"But…"

"No 'buts.' I don't want to hear any excuses. Life just doesn't happen. You must create what you want out of it."

Kelly flinched, her hand holding the cell phone suddenly going damp. She switched hands and wiped her right hand against her pajama pants. "I know. I've been thinking I should do something different with my life." Part of her wanted to make a change. The other part remained terrified.

"You know you don't love Thomas," Rachel said. "He was simply convenient."

"You're right." The room suddenly seemed cooler as if Kelly was closing a door. "I know I should take a few more risks, but I'm not good at it."

"You can do whatever you put your mind to." Kelly sensed Rachel's smile. "You're stronger than you think."

Kelly shrugged off the praise. She'd never considered herself particularly strong. "Whatever."

"Call me tomorrow? We'll talk some more."

"Yes, tomorrow."

"Good night, Kelly. And don't worry about Thomas. He's not for you."

"I know. Good night, Rachel."

Kelly ended the call and placed the iPhone on her nightstand. She sat forward and hugged her knees to her chest, resting her chin on her knees. Rachel was right. She needed change. She deserved it after all she'd been through and all the sacrifices she'd made over the years for C.B.

But Thomas Dunlap wasn't particularly the kind of change she needed.

What *did* she need? Would she always date someone who was safe?

Kelly sighed, trying to shake away her funk.

C.B. and Daniel had moved into a small house in Middletown. He was taking care of her little girl now. What if she quit her teaching job and put her things in storage? Her apartment lease was up next month. She could let the realtor sell her aunt's house. Then she'd be free to move to Lexington or maybe Northern Kentucky. At least she'd be away from the complication of Thomas.

The idea of creating a new life was new and exciting.

Yes, she'd do it. Having something to look forward to and making her mind up so quickly made her feel good.

Kelly relaxed against the pillows only to jerk forward moments later as the ringtone "My Old Kentucky Home" blared from her iPhone. *Wonderful.* Why did her mother always spoil her sweet dreams?

Kelly squeezed her eyes shut a few seconds. Then she reached over and picked up the phone. "Hi, Mother."

"Kelly, dear, how are you?"

"Fine. You're calling late."

"I need your help. With Colleen settled and school out for the year, I thought you'd have time to come home and give me a hand."

Kelly had been home once in twenty-one years and that was a year ago when her father died. She had avoided Heritage Springs, Kentucky, like the plague.

"What do you need, Mother? Is it something I can do for you from here?"

"No you can't." Her mother's voice was tight. "I'm moving out of this big house. It's too much for me. I need your help to go through things. I'm afraid I'll throw away something you or Colleen will want, you know things from your father's family."

"I don't think C.B. is interested in antiques."

"Kelly!" Her mother cut her off. "I never ask anything of you. Not since *what happened*. But now I need your help. And Colleen may want something from your father's family since she doesn't have her own father."

Ouch. Kelly should be used to her mother dredging up "the big mistake," but it hurt just the same. "Mother, I don't have time."

"You never have time." She heard her mother's deep intake of breath. "Kelly. I'm almost sixty. I don't often ask anything of you, but now I need your help."

Kelly read the pleading note in her mother's sharp voice. "With C.B. married and Aunt Bess gone, I'm starting a new life, Mother."

"I'm starting one too, dear." Her mother's tone softened. "It's just for a few weeks."

It had to be tough getting older. Aunt Bess had not taken kindly to old age and had gone kicking and screaming to the end, never acknowledging she wasn't able to do what her aging body prevented her from doing. Her mother was different. She'd never written a check until her father died. Although always subservient to him, her mother had taken his passing hard.

She and Aunt Bess could never understand Grace Baron's passivity and abject dependence on her husband. They were two self-reliant women, cut from the same cloth, and used to doing things for themselves. It was hard for them to ask for help, but they gave it freely as part of their DNA.

"Okay, Mother," Kelly said, knowing this time she couldn't deny her mother's request. "I can be up there in a couple of weeks. I have some things to get done here before then."

"You must arrive before July tenth. That's when I'm—ah—moving. Can you be here for your birthday on the sixth? It will be fun to celebrate it here."

"I'll be there. Don't worry."

As always her mother hung up without saying good-bye. Kelly slammed the iPhone down on her mattress. *Damn!* She set her jaw, flipped off the bedside lamp, and stared into the darkness. Her mother was moving into a condo or something. She needed Kelly's help, but Kelly dreaded going home.

"You can never go home again," James Agee had written. Kelly fled Heritage Springs at eighteen, accepting the truth of that adage.

By agreeing to help her mother, she was putting her life on hold one more time. Maybe Heritage Springs was as good as any place to retreat and plot her next move.

CHAPTER TWO

Heritage Springs, Kentucky
Two weeks later

Heritage Springs, Kentucky, was a small county seat in the central part of the state about seventy miles from Louisville. Kelly's arrival on Saturday, July third, coincided with the citywide Independence Day celebration on the town square.

She avoided the square and drove three blocks to her mother's house, parking in front. Turning off the ignition, Kelly stared at the two-story, white frame house with its wraparound front porch. Surrounded by a white picket fence, the house had been built in 1909 by her father's grandfather. An old-fashioned swing suspended motionless from the joists just outside a floor-to-ceiling bedroom window.

This was supposed to be home. She swallowed hard, trying to erase the needless fear she felt. Her father was dead. Memories of her harsh upbringing were just that: memories.

Because of her father's strict rules, she had never fit in with other kids. Forced to wear long skirts and put her thick, red hair up into an out-of-date bun, she was often bullied and called names. While growing up, her father had limited her friendships and activities. Later he had stopped her from dating, thinking he could prevent exactly what happened.

Taking a big breath for courage, Kelly climbed out of the car and grabbed her purse. She strode up the cracked concrete sidewalk and mounted three short steps to the front porch. A board squeaked and the heels of her sandals made flapping sounds as she crossed the wooden planks to the door. A ruled notebook paper was taped to the glass. *I'm at the square working in the cakewalk booth. Come on down. Mom.*

Kelly read her mother's scrawling handwriting and rubbed her nose. What had gotten into her "afraid of her shadow" mother? Pitching in at a charity event was contrary to her stay-at-home personality. Kelly fished for the house key in her pocket and opened the front door.

There was nothing warm and welcoming in the living room. It was filled with packing boxes that were taped and labeled. All the old comfortable furniture was gone—the worn flowered sofa from her childhood, the handcrafted cherry tables built by her grandfather, and multi-colored cotton rag rugs braided by her grandmother.

Kelly frowned. Why did her mother need her help? The packing looked to be well underway and professionally done at that.

Her breath hitched. She couldn't stay here. Regardless of its familiarity, this place had never been a true home, not like the one she and Aunt Bess had created for C.B. in Louisville.

Backing out of the room, Kelly shut the door and pocketed the key. Returning to her car, she tucked a handful of bills and her iPhone in the pocket of her khaki cropped pants, tossed her purse into the trunk, slammed it, and locked the car door.

The last thing she wanted to do was go to the Fourth of July festival where she might run into people who had known her as a kid but never accepted her—people who quickly passed judgment when she got into trouble. Granted, she had passed plenty of judgment on herself, but the criticism from busybodies didn't help matters. That had been part of the reason she left town.

ROB SCOTT SAT BALANCING on a narrow piece of hard plastic over a five-hundred-gallon, polyethylene dunk tank. A vinyl-coated steel protective cage surrounded it. Mercifully, his white T-shirt and blue swim trunks remained dry. The assorted spectators peering at him from the courthouse lawn had failed to hit the red bull's-eye which would dump him into the cold water below.

He didn't mind exposing himself like this, perching above the water, egging people on to get them to spend money on chances. Further, the more chances these people bought, the more funds he raised for the Heritage Springs Children's Club, a local organization that needed help. It had fallen on hard times over the years he had been gone from his hometown. When he returned five years ago, he had taken an interest in it, becoming a volunteer and trying to return it to the well-run club that had been there for him when he was growing up.

Rob wiped sweat off his forehead with the back of his hand. The weather was oppressive. The blistering July sun beat down on his head, and the humidity was so thick he could almost see it. Maybe a good drenching was what he needed.

"C'mon, Jake," he called out to a wide-eyed boy who attended the afterschool program and now stood smacking bubblegum in front of the tank. "Let's see you hit the bull's-eye."

"Ain't got no money, Mr. Scott," the boy replied with a shake of his head.

"Step aside, kid." A short man with a beer belly paunch under his ribbed, wife-beater undershirt edged the boy out of the way. "Your time has come, mister," the guy said with a cocky grin and proceeded to throw three baseballs, each of them missing the target.

"Ah, c'mon, buddy, you throw like a girl!" Rob shouted.

The guy paid a dollar for three more chances and missed again. He went away grumbling, but a teenage boy took his place. Rob heckled his attempt. The boy failed to connect. Maybe Rob would get through his shift without being dunked.

And then he saw her.

She stood behind a group of small girls. *Kelly?* A sharp pang took his breath away. He hadn't seen Kelly since graduation when she had given him the cold shoulder, but there was no mistaking that shock of dark red hair. She had cut it so it was short like a boy's, probably shorter than his.

He shouldn't be surprised to see her, for he knew Kelly was coming to town. In fact, he and his father planned to have dinner with Kelly and her mother tonight. Yet spotting her in the crowd, all grown up and gorgeous threw him off kilter. He didn't anticipate their meeting this way, and the shock of seeing her left him confused, an emotion he was all too familiar with lately.

Memory sliced sharply into his chest. Her father had been strict, and he didn't have the guts to run afoul of her old man. He didn't date Kelly openly. Instead they met at the library, and he walked her part of the way home, bought her Cokes, and dreamed about her at night. But he avoided her in school, taking the coward's way out.

Other boys thought Kelly was ugly. But it was the way her father made her pin up her beautiful hair and wear skirts and long-sleeved shirts as if he was trying to hide her natural beauty. Kelly was more than a pretty face. She was kind and giving and smart. And she was strong, maybe too strong for her own good.

Regret cut through him. He remembered her long, silky hair, and how he had lost himself in it that night when it slid over his bare chest. Their time together had been brief, leaving him longing for more.

"Hey, Kel," he called out to her. "Let's see that pitching arm of yours. Or has old age caught up with you?"

She stood stock-still, staring at him. She had that same piercing green-eyed gaze that intrigued him senior year. He saw her set her jaw. She dug into her pocket and paid for three balls.

"C'mon now, let's see what ya got! Wind 'er up, sugar." He played his role, egging her on.

He saw her take a steadying breath. With deliberate movements, she faced her shoulder and lower body so they lined up toward the target. Her back was perpendicular to the bull's-eye, her hips closed and pointing in the same direction. She stepped toward the target with her lead foot, pushed off her back leg, and threw the ball using her entire body.

The ball glanced harmlessly off the yellow target canvas.

"Aw, you throw like a baby," Rob chided, liking the way she threw like a boy, moving with an athletic grace that showed off her femininity. "Worse yet, you throw like a girl."

She didn't say a word, but her eyes narrowed. Lining up carefully, she threw again and this time came closer.

"Sissy! You couldn't hit a barn!" Rob rubbed it in.

She licked her lips and shook the tenseness out of her shoulders. Then she stepped forward again with the same throwing motion and sailed the hard ball toward the target.

Before he could blink, Rob felt the seat give way, and in a swift whoosh, he plunged into the dunk tank sending a splash of cold water over the side.

Damn, she did it! Rob laughed, swallowed a mouthful of water, and climbed out of the tank. He reached for a towel left in the grass next to the ladder and wiped his eyes. Toweling his hair, he walked around the side of the booth anxious to speak to Kelly.

But she was gone.

WHAT HAD SHE DONE? Kelly scurried through the crowd, sick to her stomach. Rob Scott was the last person on earth she expected to see sitting in a dunking booth on the courthouse lawn.

Her last glimpse of him was at graduation. She had avoided him after the ceremony. Already pregnant with his child, there was no way she could face him after the way his mother treated her. Besides he was bound for Northwestern the following day, heading to summer school so he could get a jump on his freshman year. Rob was like that, a risk-taker, full of big plans and lofty ambitions.

Over the years, he had attained them. She caught sketchy details of his life from her mother's gossip during visits to Louisville. Rob was a big shot lawyer in Chicago raking in millions. He had married another lawyer. That news had hurt more than she could have imagined but good for him. That's what he always wanted—career, money, and marriage. She was glad he realized his dream—something that wouldn't have happened if he had a wife and child to care for just as he was getting started.

But what was he doing here? And why did he look so damn cute and boyish sitting there in that booth? His blond hair was a little too long and his smile a little too cute. What had snapped inside her? Maybe it was when his gaze had connected with hers. That knowing, superior look in his eyes had gotten to her. Suddenly angry, remembering the way his mother had talked down to her, the way she had always felt inferior to his family, she wanted to take him down a peg—let him know there was more to her than a one-night stand.

It was a good thing she had learned the proper way to pitch so she could teach the kids in her fifth grade class. Pitching was like riding a bike. Once you had the technique, your brain and body didn't forget how to do it.

Yet she'd been surprised when the ball connected to the bull's-eye and Rob had plummeted into the tank. At that moment, she wanted to celebrate. Instead she ran.

Kelly ducked into the Country Affair Antiques Store, one of the small specialty shops that surrounded the town square, plunging deep into the rows of consigned furniture and knickknacks, not looking for anything in particular. She just hoped to hide and regain what was left of her composure.

"Kelly? Is that you?"

Kelly pasted a smile on her face as she turned and recognized Mary Beth Jameson, one of the few girls who'd talked to her in high school. "Yes, it's me," she said. "I'm surprised you knew me."

"There's no mistaking that hair color. I like it short." Mary Beth gave her a quick hug. "I'm so glad to see you. I figured you would come home."

Kelly stepped back, crossing her arms even though the cool air-conditioned shop felt good. Town gossips already knew her mother was moving. "Yes, I'm here to help my mother."

"I hear congratulations are in order," Mary Beth said. "When I saw your mother in church last Sunday, she told me her good news and mentioned your daughter got married recently."

Kelly smiled. She was proud of C.B. and her marriage to such a nice young man. "Thank you. How's your family?" She couldn't remember if Mary Beth was married.

"My parents retired to Florida," Mary Beth said, "and my twin sons start college in the fall."

"Imagine us having grown children." Kelly shook her head in disbelief.

Mary Beth huffed a breath as if disgusted. "I turned forty in February, and I tell you, I feel so old."

"Well, you don't look it," Kelly said giving her an approving glance. Mary Beth looked the same as the last day she saw her—the day Kelly had said goodbye before boarding the bus for Louisville to live with Aunt Bess.

"Phaw!" Mary Beth waved off the compliment. "I camouflage the fat well. You, on the other hand, still look trim and fit."

"I work at it." Kelly shrugged. They turned and strolled toward the shop door.

"You're not the only one who works at it," Mary Beth remarked. "I see Rob Scott jogging every morning on the high school track. He's still as handsome as he was in high school."

Kelly paused at the door, took a breath, and fought the pain that shot through her heart. She glanced sideways at Mary Beth wondering if her friend had ever guessed the truth. "What's Rob doing back in Heritage Springs?"

"He's working in his Dad's law firm, *and* he's divorced."

The news rocked Kelly like a blast of wind. "Really?" She tried to sound nonchalant.

Mary Beth leaned close. "It was a nasty one," she said in a loud whisper. Then she stood straight, her face reflecting satisfaction about the juicy tidbits she was about to impart. "They had moved from Chicago several years ago, but his wife never liked Heritage Springs. She up and left him for another man."

Kelly stepped back, floored by the information. "She did?"

Mary Beth nodded. "Yes. Rumor says Rob is doing a lot of work for the children's club because he's trying to avoid dealing with the loss of his wife."

"Really? He must have loved her very much." Kelly looked away, confused. She didn't know how to digest all that gossip. The fact that Rob was back in town was reason to finish with her mother's business ASAP and leave. Thinking Heritage Springs could be a cozy retreat had been a big fat mistake.

Mary Beth opened the shop door. Light streamed inside revealing dust motes dancing in the summertime air. "Well, I've got to run. So nice to see you again."

"It's been nice seeing you," Kelly agreed. *And informative.* Knowing that she could run into Rob again didn't do much for her equilibrium.

She turned and wandered down the nearest aisle, trying to make sense of Mary Beth's revelation. She had nothing to fear from seeing Rob again. C.B. was healthy and happy and all grown up. No one in the whole wide world knew her secret. She'd kept it well hidden. If she stayed away from Rob Scott, he could pose no serious problem.

Kelly rounded a corner and halted. Rob walked down the opposite aisle looking as if he was searching for something...or someone. She stepped back behind a huge mahogany armoire. *Great.* If she had nothing to worry about, why was her heart racing?

"There you are."

Kelly's blood stilled. She turned slowly, reluctantly, and stared up at a practically naked ghost from her past. Rob's wet T-shirt had the Heritage Springs Children's Club logo on it. He wore swim trunks and Teva sandals. His dark, blond hair, still damp, curled at the nape of his neck and around his ears, too long for a high-priced Chicago lawyer she thought.

Tall, bronzed, muscled—he was much more than her faded dreams. His presence was magnetic. Kelly felt the pull of his charisma, his blue eyes drawing her in, even though he had not said more than three words.

"Sorry about that," she said, hardly able to speak, and nodded at him to indicate she meant his wet clothes.

"You're the first one to dunk me all day," he said as she felt heat sweep her face. "I must admit I was feeling pretty cocky about avoiding the water."

"You were always a cocky son-of-a-gun."

He grinned. "And you always surprised me when you spoke your mind in class."

Kelly shrugged, amazed how easy it was talking to this specter from her past. "I hope I've learned a little caution over the years. My mouth doesn't get me into as much trouble as it used to."

"We had some hot debates in journalism class," Rob acknowledged, his gaze sweeping over her face.

"That we did." Kelly offered an awkward smile and glanced away, unable to meet his probing eyes. *Damn!* In three days, she would be forty. She was not a heartsick teenager. The promise of passion in Rob's eyes, however unintentional, was almost too overwhelming to be ignored, and it made her queasy.

"You disappeared after I got dunked," Rob said. "Luckily, I ran into Mary Beth, and she told me where to find you."

"Oh?" Good old Mary Beth. She had certainly taken over as queen of the town gossips. Her friend was probably already spreading the word that divorced, hunky lawyer Rob Scott was inquiring about unfortunate Kelly Baron, the poor girl from town who got knocked up in high school and never married.

Why so defensive all of a sudden? Plenty of women were in her shoes. And there weren't old maids in the twenty-first century. A woman wasn't a failure simply because she never married. At least, she had made a conscious decision about her marital status, letting Thomas down as easily as she could before leaving Louisville, never taking his ring. She was liberated. And she liked it that way.

There was nothing to be defensive about.

Except when she stood face-to-face with the father of her child, who was now divorced and even more drop-dead gorgeous all grown up.

"How did you make that great throw?" he asked.

"I'm just lucky, I guess." She tried to brush him off.

But it didn't work.

"I'm glad I'm going to get time to spend with you. You can teach me how to pitch like that so I can teach the children's club kids."

"We're spending time together?" This was news.

"We're going to dinner at the Eagle's Nest tonight. You know, I want to feel good about this marriage. I haven't had much luck with the institution myself." Rob cocked his head and she saw something like hurt in his eyes. "But the two of them are dead set on doing it. How do you feel about it?"

"About what?" Somewhere along the line he had lost her. Had she missed something in the conversation? Kelly frowned, her lips turning down. "I'm sorry. I don't know what you're talking about, Rob. Who is 'we'?"

"You, your mom, my dad, and me," he answered quickly.

"I don't know your dad. Why are we going to dinner?"

"To talk about wedding plans."

"What wedding?" Kelly heard the pitch in her voice rise.

He rubbed his forehead. "Don't you know? Your mom is marrying my dad."

CHAPTER THREE

"I can't believe you didn't tell me." Kelly poured microwaved water into a crockery mug over an Earl Gray teabag. Trying to still her shaking hand, she pressed the flat part of a spoon against the bag while the tea steeped. She was so angry she couldn't look her mother in the face.

Grace Baron brought a small glass pitcher filled with half-and-half to the kitchen table and sat down across from her daughter. The kitchen was the only place in the house to sit, and even it was crowded with big brown boxes packed with her mother's dishes and pots and pans.

"You were so busy with Colleen's wedding and the end of school," Grace said with a shrug. She put her elbows on the table and leaned toward Kelly. "I didn't want to bother you."

"Bother me?" Kelly couldn't believe what she'd just heard. She looked up. "About something so important? You let me believe you were moving into a condo."

"I never said anything about a condo. You assumed that's what I was doing."

"That's what women your age usually do when they downsize, not get married!"

"I'm not dead yet." Her mother's mouth drew into an angry straight line. "It's never too late to find true love."

Kelly ran her fingers through her short-cropped hair. "How long have you known this man?"

Grace shifted uneasily in her chair but didn't remove her gaze from her daughter. "*His* name is Howard. I've known *of* him since your father and I moved to Heritage Springs, but I didn't meet him personally until this year. We met at the grief support group at church," Grace quickly explained, her chin lifting as if to deflect Kelly's implicit criticism. "He was lonely. His second wife died two years ago."

"Second wife?" Kelly's voice rose.

"Yes." Grace drew the word out losing patience. "His first wife, Rob's mother, died when Rob was in his early twenties."

At the mention of Rob's name, Kelly stiffened. She was wired tight. Her right heel tapped silently against the hardwood floor. She cupped the mug in her hands and took a sip, forcing herself to ease the strain in her shoulders as she stared across the table at a mother she didn't recognize anymore.

At least, Rob's domineering mother was no longer in the picture.

"Even though your father was a harsh man, I depended on him." Glancing down, Grace toyed with the handle of the cream pitcher. "I'm not like you, Kelly. You don't need a man. You're okay not being married. But I've never lived alone."

Hearing herself described that way made Kelly grimace inwardly. Her mother's portrayal wasn't flattering. She wasn't independent or self-reliant by choice. She liked to think of herself as a woman who had done what she had to do.

"You sell yourself short, Mother," Kelly said, unable to hide her frown.

"I don't think so." Grace was defensive. "Your father is not around to help me. Neither are you. I can't do all this on my own." She waved her hand around the kitchen. "This house is too big for a single person "

Kelly's eyes narrowed as she stared at the tiny woman with salt and pepper gray hair. When she told her parents about her pregnancy, her father had been furious. He had insisted on an abortion. Her mother, always the good wife, had not objected, leaving Kelly alone to defend herself from the wrath of a man sorely disappointed in his only daughter. She had never gotten over her mother's betrayal.

Kelly placed the mug on the table and leaned forward. "I don't understand." She shook her head. "Why Mr. Scott? He's not our kind. We're a blue-collar family. The Scotts are from Locust Grove."

It was true. The Scotts were Heritage Springs' high society unlike Kelly's father who had worked a minimum wage job at a plastics injection molding company. The Barons lived in a fairly nice house only because her dad had inherited it. The Scott family lived in a stately colonial in the better part of town. Howard Scott was a lawyer and former town mayor.

And he was C.B.'s grandfather.

The thought made Kelly choke. She coughed, swallowed hard, and looked away. Good grief. What was happening here? This was developing into her worst nightmare.

Grace started to cry. She got up and pulled a tissue from a box on the counter and then came back to her chair. "I can't believe you're worried about appearances." She dabbed the corner of her eye. "That's so unlike you."

Another dig at her big mistake. Would she ever live it down?

"Howie isn't a bit concerned about what people think," Grace said.

Howie? Kelly sank back in her chair. *Think!* This was going to happen—she could tell from the uncharacteristic determination in her mother's weepy eyes. How could she protect C.B.? Herself? Facing the hard edge of reality had her searching for an escape.

"What do you want from me, Mother? Why am I here?"

"I knew you wouldn't come if I told you the truth." Grace wiped her nose. "You and C.B. and Daniel are family. I wanted my family to be here with me when I marry Howie. Don't you understand, Kelly? Howie makes me better. I can be myself when I'm with him."

Kelly sat forward again. She should feel guilty that her mother had to trick her own daughter into coming to her wedding. But she had finished with the list of "shoulds" a long time ago.

"When is it?" Kelly asked in a cool voice.

"July ninth. Until then, I really do need your help going through things. I've left your room for you to do." Grace nodded, her eyes watering. "And the attic is a mess."

"Okay." Kelly sat back widening the distance between them. "What about this dinner tonight?"

"I want you to meet Howie. We're invited to dinner with his son. You remember Rob from high school. He's divorced now *and* single."

Divorced people were usually single, but Kelly didn't point that out. Instead, gritting her teeth, she remained silent. A smart-alecky comment wasn't worth the effort. Her mother was matchmaking, and Kelly was being set up. *With Rob Scott of all people.* The irony was too much.

"You'd best clean up," Grace said. "Put on something besides those shorts."

Now her mother sounded like her normal self. Kelly pushed back from the table and stood. "Yes, that sounds like a good idea." Giving her mother a tiny smile, she went into the living room where she'd left her suitcase.

She slung her duffle bag over her shoulder and grabbed the handle of her wheeled luggage. Then she climbed the stairs to her childhood room, dragging the luggage behind her.

Kelly dropped the duffle bag onto the wooden floor by her bedroom door. Slowly she released her grip on the handle of her luggage, leaving the bag at the doorway, and stepped into the room. A flood of shame overcame her. She sucked in a breath and stared at her bedroom. It looked the same as it had looked over twenty years ago when she was a kid in trouble.

For one heart-stopping moment, Kelly felt as if she had never left home. All the guilt and anger and fear from those last two months of high school came spiraling back. Her knees weakened, and she sank down on her Jenny Lind bed with its white spindle headboard and pink and purple flowered bedspread. Why had her mother refused to change this room?

Last year when she came for her father's funeral, she and C.B. had stayed at a motel. She hadn't even been up to her room. Now seeing it again like this was creepy, especially after running into Rob today. Memories rushed back as she sat quietly looking at a Phantom of the Opera poster that had yellowed on the wall.

Kelly reached for a chubby Cabbage Patch Kid doll propped against her pillow shams. Gathering the curly-haired doll up in her arms, she hugged it as if the embrace could ease the hurt of the past or free her from the fear of discovery.

Deep down Kelly regretted her lapse in judgment and lack of control that night so long ago. Afraid to involve him because of his mother's warning, Kelly wasn't sure if Rob would have turned out to be the knight in shining armor to rescue her from her mistake. She knew though that she couldn't have borne the disappointment if he had rejected her too.

Yet C.B. had come from their blunder. She didn't regret her daughter—only the things that could have been if she had made different choices.

"Oh, God!" Kelly gasped unable to choke back the tears flowing freely for the first time in years. She hugged the doll and gazed at the faded poster. "I don't believe this," she said to the quiet room. "This is not happening."

She was scared, fearing losing control. Her life and C.B.'s lay in the balance the next few days. Her eyelids drooped and her mouth pulled downward as she fought the tense knot in her stomach.

If her mother married Rob's father, how was she going to keep her secret? It had been with her like a living thing for twenty-one years.

CHAPTER FOUR

Saturday evening

"Rob, you're an incurable romantic," his ex-wife Jessica had told him soon after they met. Maybe that's why he had blindly ignored the warning signs in their marriage until it was too late, and why, even after what had happened, he was happy for his dad.

Rob stood on the broken sidewalk, one foot resting on the bottom step to the porch, and watched his sixty-six-year-old father embrace Grace Baron. At his dad's knock, she had rushed out of her front door and into his open arms, apparently oblivious to the world around her. Their public display of affection embarrassed Rob. He looked away toward the shaded street peppered with white picket fences and turn-of-the-twentieth-century houses.

A widower, his father deserved what pleasure and contentment marriage to Mrs. Baron would bring. He had buried two wives, after all, Rob thought glancing back. He was impressed by the older man's willingness to start over. And from what he knew about his future stepmother's joyless first marriage, Rob figured she too had earned a bit of happiness.

He shouldn't be too eager to try it again. Jessica had burned him badly. But the risk-taker optimist within him longed for a second chance. Maybe being an incurable romantic wasn't smart for a lawyer who had to deal with hard facts. In his personal life, the constant push-pull of dream versus reality had proven to be a constant plague.

"Someone will take off your rose-colored glasses," Jessica had warned early on.

She should know since she was the one who did it.

Rob continued up the steps as Kelly came to the door and froze doe-like, her eyes wide with alarm. He couldn't blame her reaction. It must feel strange for Kelly to see her mother in the arms of a man not her father.

"Are you two lovebirds going to break it up?" he asked, hoping to add levity to an awkward moment.

Of course, the two only had eyes for each other. They missed the uncomfortable look on Kelly's face and the way she hung back as if afraid to leave the safety of the house.

Rob was keenly aware of Kelly. He sensed her uneasiness and something more. Fear. Was she alarmed to discover her mother's upcoming marriage? He learned today that Grace, for whatever reason, had neglected to be honest with her daughter. He only hoped his dad wasn't walking into a family situation beyond his ability to control.

The two lovebirds drew apart but continued holding hands.

"Kelly, dear, come meet Howie," Grace said, urging her daughter forward by extending her free hand.

Kelly took a step outside. She wore a flattering white sleeveless sundress that showed off her tanned skin. Rob's eyes were automatically drawn to the fitted bust and the waistline that hit beneath it —empire style he thought it was called. The skirt flowed from there, ending above Kelly's knees. His gaze traveled down her shapely bronze legs to strappy white sandals. He slowly lifted his gaze back up again to her eyes.

My God! What a far cry from the dowdy schoolgirl he had once known. To say his interest was piqued was the understatement of the year.

Not many women her age could wear such a dress. Jessica certainly couldn't. She was always fighting her weight. And Kelly's short-cropped red hair that softly framed her face made her look even younger than her almost forty years.

Her gaze shifted from the couple to Rob and back again, and then she pasted a smile on her lips to cover the shadow of annoyance that crossed her face.

"Howie, this is Kelly, my daughter. You've heard me speak of her." Grace was anxious, Rob could tell, but she put on a proud smile.

His dad was his gracious self, dropping Grace's hand and clasping Kelly's in a welcoming handshake. "I'm pleased to meet you," he said, his words friendly.

"Nice to meet you."

Rob wondered if she meant it.

There was an air of hostility about her. And mystery. Rob figured no one but Kelly and he knew about their one night in the backseat of a car. At the time, their secret friendship had seemed important —all those clandestine meetings at the library, the handholding and whispered conversation culminating in that night of sex.

Sneaking around had been exciting, partly because Kelly's father had an authoritarian reputation and partly because his friends would be shocked if they knew. It had started out as a lark, talking to the "nun" at the library. But there was nothing nun-like about her Rob had found out.

And never forgotten.

"You look lovely tonight, Kelly," he said to her.

He was eager to get to know her again. There was something intriguing about sharing a secret with her, even one as harmless as a one-night stand over twenty years earlier.

KELLY'S STOMACH twisted and she viewed Rob with mistrust. "Thanks. You clean up pretty good yourself," she said unable to come back with anything wittier.

This nightmare didn't quit. First she had run into Rob, and then she'd found out her mother was engaged to be married. Now Rob's father was holding hands with her mother like a man head over heels in love. There was something off-putting about the whole thing. Of course, most people would think it charming and sweet for two old people to find love again.

No one knew what Kelly knew. And no one could understand her fear.

"Let's not stand out in this heat," Howie suggested. "I don't want my little flower to wilt."

Grace giggled, and Kelly thought she would gag. She glanced at Rob who winked as if he understood her predicament.

"I've gotten used to it," Rob whispered as they followed their parents to Howie's Lexus SUV. "They're very happy together."

Kelly wasn't ready to admit her feelings out loud; although she suspected her body language gave her away. "I thought you had misgivings."

"A few, but I figure there's nothing I can do to stop them even if I wanted to."

Wonderful. This disaster was going to happen.

Rob handed Kelly into the backseat while his father helped her mother into the passenger side. Rob shut her door and came around to the other side, climbing in beside her.

Their closeness was unnerving. Kelly fought down the flaring panic that rose in her chest and made her feel like throwing up.

"I hope you like this restaurant." Rob's attempt at small talk was pathetic.

"I'm sure I will." Kelly hoped her lack of interest would shut him up.

Sitting in the backseat with Rob was eerie. She had stepped into a time warp. Twenty-one years ago, she and Rob had shared the backseat of another of his father's cars. Kelly shifted nervously on the bench seat, feeling the leather's coolness against her exposed back. Glancing at him, she caught recognition lighting his eyes. Rob remembered too.

"This seems oddly familiar," Rob said under his breath.

Her mother and Howie were chatting, oblivious to the occupants of the backseat. Still Kelly didn't want to go where Rob was going.

"I don't know what you're talking about." She looked out the window trying to signal an end to the conversation.

"Come on. You can't have forgotten."

She turned quickly, her senses alert. "There are a lot of things I haven't forgotten." Her voice was too sharp, her breath coming fast.

Kelly didn't need his probing or the allusion to their past.

"Easy now," he cautioned. "I didn't mean to touch a sore spot."

"Well, you have, and I appreciate you not talking about it. It's been a long time. We don't need the past interfering with the next few days. We have to get along for their sakes." She nodded toward the front seat and their parents.

"Point taken."

Rob turned his head to look out his window. They rode in silence the rest of the way, listening to Grace discuss the strawberry wedding cake June Hobson was baking for the occasion.

A LOCAL FAMILY had purchased The Eagle's Nest Grist Mill several years earlier. They had stocked a pond with trout and another one with catfish and turned the old mill into a restaurant serving fried fish, fries, hush puppies, and coleslaw.

The meal was tasty, but Kelly, having no appetite, only picked at the catfish. Her mother, on the other hand, had never been so jovial. Kelly was surprised by the change in the woman. Granted, she was free from the confines of a dysfunctional marriage, but there was something more to her mother's new happiness, and it had everything to do with Rob's father. Kelly listened half-heartedly to their talk of wedding plans and tried to avoid eye contact with Rob.

After a desert of key lime pie and coffee, Howie asked, "Care to take a walk around the pond?"

"It's much too hot for me, Howie, dear," Grace said. "Why don't the two young people go on?"

Matchmaking. Kelly didn't need to be a mind reader to figure out her mother's not so subtle motive.

She pushed back her chair, and it scraped on the plank floor. Rob jumped to his feet and held the cane back chair for her. *Ah, the perfect gentleman.* Kelly bristled at his thoughtfulness, knowing she was being foolish. She walked ahead of him down the winding steps and out into the heavy twilight of a hot July day.

The restaurant was in a log cabin built next to the nineteenth century era mill. Kelly stopped beside the mill trace and listened to the slap-slap sound of the water-powered paddle as it turned in slow rhythm. The air smelled of heat, frying fish, and wet, moss-covered wood.

Rob came up behind. Her skin prickled.

"It was a different time," he mused aloud.

Kelly let out a long breath, annoyed that he aroused fears and uncertainties. "Life was harder," she stated simply.

"But there was honesty about it." His voice remained thoughtful. "When life was about basic survival, it was less complicated."

"Seems to me, life continues to be about survival." Kelly stepped away, trying to shut down any conversation between them.

Rob wasn't so easily put off. He followed, and they strolled silently together along the gravel path beside the catfish pond until they came to an empty bench on the other side.

"Let's sit down and watch the sun go down," he suggested.

Kelly hesitated but then sat down, scooting to the edge of the wooden bench as Rob sat beside her. The last time she'd shared a bench with a man, he had proposed. *Another of this night's ironies.*

In the western sky, the sun was an orange splotch immersed in the hazy heat of the evening. They sat quietly a few minutes.

"I've wondered why you never married," Rob remarked casually.

"I never found the right person...unlike you," Kelly responded. She knew her reply was insensitive, but she didn't like being put on the spot and couldn't keep the irritation from her voice.

"I'm not sure I believe in the 'right person.'"

There was so much hurt in Rob's soft response that Kelly glanced at him.

He searched her face. "What about your baby's father? Did he step up to the plate?"

Fear cut right through her. "No." The lie rolled from her tongue with ease. She'd had plenty of practice. "I raised C.B. with the help of my great-aunt."

"What a bastard," Rob muttered under his breath. He looked at her. "If that had been my child, I would have stepped up."

"Really?"

"You sound skeptical."

She glared at him and blew out an unladylike snort. "I couldn't depend on my parents. They didn't even 'step up.' So why should I trust your empty words?" Kelly glanced down. "It's a moot point anyway."

"I have no business asking you about your life," he said and then added with a sly grin, "but I must admit you intrigue me."

She laughed mirthlessly to cover her annoyance. "We hardly know anything about each other. We were different people twenty years ago."

"You're right." He let out a breath. "It's just that riding with you brought back a rash of old memories. Good ones, I must admit."

"Memories are inexact things."

"I suppose so." Rob lapsed into silence.

Danger signals clamored in Kelly's head. Only a few more discussions like this and Rob might put two and two together—backseat, Kelly leaves town, pregnancy. It wasn't hard to figure out knowing what Rob knew. He was the only one who had all the puzzle pieces, the only one who could guess her secret.

"There's your father waving at us." Kelly stood up, glad for the distraction. "We'd better go."

As she had done in the past, Kelly ran away from an uncomfortable situation.

CHAPTER FIVE

Sunday morning

As she showered and dressed, Kelly mulled over the events of the previous day. Sure, she and Rob had a past, but it wasn't as glorious and idyllic as he wanted to remember. Not coming clean about their daughter didn't trouble her. Her loyalty lay with C.B., not with a man whose only contribution to her child's life had been a one-night stand.

Was she being selfish? Probably, but twenty-one years ago she had reasons for keeping quiet. The secret had been a huge part of her life, something she kept without thinking just as she ate or breathed.

Kelly went downstairs to the kitchen, her steps reluctant. The house was too quiet, tomb-like with its silent packing boxes blocking the way. Howie was paying for the move. It figured because her mother didn't have that kind of money.

Kelly sighed as she tried to quell the trepidation that churned in her stomach. She didn't like change and she was getting a double dose of it at the moment.

In the kitchen Kelly discovered that her mother had started a pot of coffee. Under a clean mug on the countertop was a note that read "gone to church."

"Church?" Kelly poured coffee into the mug and took a welcome first sip. When had her mother started going to church? This was a change. *Another thing to view with suspicion.*

A "Danny Boy" ringtone shattered the quiet. "C.B." Kelly pulled her lips up into a slight smile, her heart filling with warmth, and set down her mug. She picked up her iPhone and swiped the slider across the bottom of the display to answer the phone. "Hello, pumpkin."

"So, Mom, what do you think about Gran?" C.B.'s soft voice was high pitched with excitement.

"You know?"

"Sure." Kelly heard her daughter laugh. "She told me last week but swore me to secrecy."

"She told *you?*" Kelly couldn't control her surprise.

"She's so happy. Gran said she couldn't keep the news to herself any longer."

"Why didn't she tell me?" And why did her mother let her learn it from Rob Scott, of all people? The affront stung. "She lied to get me here," Kelly said, knowing her protest sounded petty.

"You know you wouldn't have gone to Heritage Springs if she'd told you the truth," C.B. pointed out as if she were a mother scolding a child.

"That's not true."

"Oh, don't be so defensive."

"I'm not defensive!"

"I can hear it in your voice. You never were a good liar."

Kelly sat down hard on one of the two remaining kitchen chairs. Her daughter was laughing at her. She sucked in a deep calming breath. "I guess you're right."

"Daniel and ⁻ will be up for the wedding on the ninth. Try to find out what Gran wants for a gift, will you?"

"I haven't a clue." A bridal gift was the last thing on Kelly's mind.

"Well, anyway, I've thought about buying her something sexy and red. Something to spice up her wedding night."

"C.B.!" Kelly heard more laughter. Her daughter was enjoying her discomfort as much as she enjoyed her grandmother's forthcoming nuptials.

"We'll see you then, Mom," C.B. said. "And don't be upset. Relax and be happy for her. She deserves it."

"We'll see," she said as C.B. rung off. Standing up, Kelly returned to the kitchen sink, picked up her mug and dumped the coffee down the drain. "Damn."

She needed help—a way to get out of this sticky situation—but with C.B. and Daniel coming to town, she was trapped. She couldn't give them any reason to suspect the extent of her dilemma.

Kelly glanced at her iPhone to check the time. Then heading into the hall, she touched the contact button for Rachel.

"You've got to be kidding me!" Rachel's first reaction mirrored Kelly's. At least, someone understood.

With her iPhone clamped to her ear, Kelly mounted the stairs to the second floor then the narrow flight to the attic.

"I thought I was coming home to help my mother move into a condo," Kelly told her best friend. "Instead, she's getting married. 'It's never too late to find true love' she told me."

Rachel gave a short laugh. "You must admit the woman has guts."

"I don't know when she got them." Kelly shook her head. "She certainly didn't have any when she was married to my father."

"In my experience, knowing you're truly loved is a liberating thing," Rachel said. "You can be yourself easier if you have that assurance."

"I wouldn't know." No, she wouldn't. Kelly fought a deep resentment. Anger at Rob for not being the man she needed back then made her heart pound. Anger at the impotent fear that gripped her and caused her to date men like Thomas Dunlap.

"Your mother must feel very secure to make this change."

"I guess." Kelly stood at the threshold to the attic and told Rachel all the gory details, leaving out the part about Rob and the fact that C.B. was Howie's granddaughter.

"I assume she's moving in with Howie once they're married. What's going to happen to her house?" Rachel asked.

"I don't know." Kelly switched on the overhead light bulb and walked across the hardwood floor skirting the old furniture draped with sheets and dusty boxes of junk stacked on top of other boxes of junk. A dirty window allowed a glimmer of weak summer sunlight into the area under the steeped roof.

"Wouldn't it be fun if you turned her house into a bed and breakfast? Carl and I have enjoyed owning ours, and you were searching for something different to do with your life."

"It's not that simple." No, and it wasn't safe. Kelly couldn't chance staying in Heritage Springs any longer than necessary.

"Well, think about it. Anything is doable, if you want it badly enough."

"That's just it. I don't know what I want."

"You'll find out."

Rachel's words were reassuring, but Kelly wasn't willing to be reassured. There was too much at stake. They talked a few minutes longer then ended the call.

Kelly stuffed her iPhone into the pocket of her denim shorts and took stock of the attic. With no air conditioning up here, it wasn't likely she'd spend much time sorting and packing. Best to drag the boxes downstairs somehow. But where to start?

Wandering over to the window, she gazed down at the yard below. How many times as a child had she run through the yard with other kids from the neighborhood? They'd played hide and seek and once during time off from school, they'd built snow forts and held mock wars—boys against girls—throwing snowballs and freezing their butts off.

She had friends at one time. That was before she became an outcast. Before her father made her wear ugly dresses and pin up her hair. Kelly squeezed her eyes shut remembering that time. Her father had gone weird, yelling at her and accusing her of things she had never done. Was she ten at the time? Or eleven? Or maybe she was twelve and had just gotten her period.

Sometimes she used to escape up here to the attic. Not in the summer, but in the fall and spring. Sometimes in the winter if it wasn't too cold. She'd read up here, sitting on the old, wooden footlocker under the window.

Kelly opened her eyes and glanced down. The footlocker, the one her grandfather had used during World War II, was in the same spot and still locked with the padlock she had put on it in high school. The attic looked the same. So did her room. She was almost forty years old and today she felt like a kid again—a scared, unhappy kid. The pain and bewilderment of that lost time gnawed at her in a tragically familiar way.

Why was it when everyone around her was changing she felt stuck? As if she was marking time, neither coming nor going, just being.

Swallowing hard, Kelly fought back tears of self-pity, swaying a little as she stood in the middle of the attic floor. This wasn't like her. She didn't cry. She didn't feel sorry for herself. She got on with things. Did what had to be done. Made the best of bad situations.

Just like she had to do now.

"Kelly!"

Her mother's sharp voice rang out, drifting up the stairs all the way to the attic. Kelly couldn't escape it.

"Upstairs, Mother," she called down.

"Good. I've brought Rob home with me. He's offered to help us clean out the attic."

CHAPTER SIX

Kelly wanted to sink through the hardwood floor, but she refused to let her insecurity get the best of her. Instead she drew a deep breath and waited. Not for long. Rob bounded up the stairs. His presence in the hot, dark attic, wearing only shorts and a T-shirt, was like that of a celestial angel—bright and vibrant, as glowing as the smile on his face.

He stopped and stared at her. She stood a little straighter, a knot tightening in her stomach. Their gazes connected and sizzled.

Kelly heard her mother's laboring steps coming up the stairs. She swallowed hard. "What?"

"You're beautiful," he said as if he really meant it.

Kelly glanced down at her white T-shirt, denim shorts, and white sandals. Who was he kidding? She snapped her head up and glared at him, not trusting herself to speak.

"There you are." Her mother had words enough for both of them. Having come from church, she was dressed in a conservative blue suit and a soft white blouse, looking better than Kelly remembered.

"What a mess this place is." Grace shouldered past them, shaking her head, as she walked to the middle of the room. The lone light bulb threw her face into sharp contrast. "It's hot. We certainly can't work up here."

"That's what I was thinking," Rob flexed his bare arm, showing off his biceps. "You need male help."

"Show off." Kelly turned with a huff, unable to look at the exposed reminder of his male body. "You can take this footlocker downstairs, but leave it in my room. I'll sort through it there."

"Kelly, don't be rude," her mother scolded.

"That's okay, Grace." Rob crossed to the window and lifted the footlocker with ease. "Kel will get used to having me around. She has to since she's going to be my stepsister."

WHAT? Kelly turned quickly to see Rob's hunky backside as he left the attic lugging the footlocker. The nightmare was growing more horrible by the moment.

"Really, Kelly, why are you acting this way toward Rob? He's only here to help."

Kelly closed her eyes a moment in an attempt to control her exasperation. No wonder she never wanted to come home. Here she remained a child.

"There are a lot of things I shouldn't do, Mother, but that has never stopped me."

"I just want us to get along." Her mother shook her head, her eyes hopeful. "I just want us to be a family."

"This is *your* family. *Your* idea. I'll try to be polite, but don't count on me liking it." Kelly snatched up a tattered box and marched down the stairs, sidestepping Rob who was coming up. Their shoulders brushed, and Kelly jerked away quickening her pace.

"Be careful," he called after her.

"I'm not a child!" *Good grief.* Now Rob treated her like one.

At that moment, her foot slipped on the next to the bottom step, and still clutching the box, she bumped on her butt down the remaining two steps.

"Damn," she cried out in anger. "Damn! Damn! Damn!"

"Good catch."

Kelly glanced over her shoulder and lifted her gaze up the flight of stairs to see a pair of hairy legs and tan cargo shorts with a very male bulge that left nothing to the imagination. Her view wouldn't be so bad during normal circumstances, but circumstances were not normal. This was Rob, and he was laughing at her.

KELLY DIDN'T KNOW how cute she looked sprawled out on the floor giving him the evil eye. If he were a gentleman, he'd rush downstairs and lift the box from her arms, but he was enjoying himself too much. Rob loved her spunk—maybe it went with the red hair —and he loved the way she'd overcome the straightjacket her father had put her in as a kid.

It took strength for her to raise a child by herself. He admired her for that. Kelly's self-sacrifice put her on a pedestal in his eyes.

For the first time since his divorce, he was ready to try again. He'd been licking his wounds too long. There wasn't anyone in Heritage Springs worth dating. The hot women were all married, and the single women didn't interest him. Not like Kelly with her flashing green eyes and quick temper.

"Stay put. I'll help you up." Rob trotted down the steps and picked up the box. It wasn't heavy. Just awkward.

"Thanks."

He pulled her to her feet with his free hand, his fingers locking with hers, not letting them go. Face-to-face, her expression stricken, Rob held her against his chest for a heart-beating moment.

"Think you'll live?" He winked at her.

"This time."

Kelly wrenched her hand from his and turned away flouncing back up the attic stairs. Rob watched her go, appreciating the view. Miss Baron could play hard to get all she wanted, but in various circles, he was known for his persistence. She didn't stand a chance.

Unable to hide a smug grin, he delivered the box to an open space on the living room floor and went back for more. He passed Kelly several times on the stairs as they carried boxes up and down. She tried to ignore him, but he could tell she was working too hard at it. He was getting under her skin, which suited him just fine.

WHO CALLED A TRUCE? Kelly certainly hadn't, but for some odd and very strange reason, she and Rob worked together during the afternoon. He kept a deliberate, taunting distance, and Kelly was only too glad to let him, very proud of the control she exhibited. In fact, she seemed to have the whole situation in hand. Rob Scott was not going to get to her. That part of her life was over and done with.

By four o'clock the living room was organized chaos. Boxes of donation items were collected in the middle of the room. Mismatched chairs and an old oak table were shoved against a wall ready for the second hand store. The trashcans behind the house were overflowing and boxes of trash were stacked beside them.

"Are you sure you don't want anything?" Her mother asked in a voice reflecting her disappointment.

"No." Kelly shook her head. "I'm not the sentimental type."

"If you can keep this stuff here until the children's club yard sale in September, we can use the items," Rob said.

Was he really serious about his volunteer work for the children's club? Kelly bit her lower lip and assessed Rob with a questioning glance. "You can sell this junk?"

"You'd be surprised how much will sell. What's the old saying? One man's junk is another man's treasure."

Rachel's earlier question came to mind, and Kelly turned to her mother. "What *are* you going to do with the house?"

"Sell it too, I guess. Howie and I have talked about it since you don't seem to want it."

The hurt in her mother's voice was palpable. "What makes you say that?" Kelly asked.

"Well, do you?"

Kelly's eyes narrowed and she looked away unable to meet her mother's challenge. "I don't know what I want." She turned and left the living room. "I'm going to get some fresh air."

Outside on the porch, she sat down on the swing, tucking her feet up under her cross-legged. She had come to Heritage Springs thinking her mother needed her. Since C.B.'s marriage no one needed her, and for a woman who had fashioned her whole life giving to her child and later her aunt, it was a traumatic loss. The whole idea of creating a new life and "finding herself" was no longer appealing. In two more days, she'd be forty. Why didn't she know herself already, for heaven's sakes? Shouldn't she have her life together by now?

Rob came out of the house carrying two tall glasses of pink lemonade. He stopped in front of her, looking down, and extended a glass. "Your mother made this."

Kelly uncrossed her legs and put her bare feet on the floor. Sometime during the afternoon she'd kicked off her sandals. "Thanks." She took the glass from him. It was wet from condensation.

Rob sat down beside her, the swing moving with his weight. It was much smaller than the bench beside the fishpond, and their shoulders touched with an intimacy Kelly didn't want. She drank the sweetly tart lemonade, biding time and controlling her sharp intake of breath and rising pulse.

"Why did you ask your mother about the house?" Rob wanted to know. "Are you thinking about staying in Heritage Springs?"

"No." Kelly studied the glass. She moved it and watched the ice cubes twirl. "My friend and her husband have a bed and breakfast. She mentioned the idea to me today about turning this old house into one."

"This town could certainly use more guest space. I might be interested in investing in it, if you decide to stay." Rob took a long sip. Then he held the glass loosely in his hands and resting his elbows on his knees, he stared at the floor. "It's not a bad place, our hometown. I've grown to love it again."

Kelly stiffened, memories closing in on her. "Well, I don't think I fit in here."

"My wife said that…my ex-wife," he amended. "Jess is nothing like you, but you were born here, Kel. I can understand why you left, because of your daughter, but I think you'd fit in here just fine, if you came back."

"Well, it's not as if my mother has need of my help." There was an edge of hurt in her voice. Why could that be? She was the one who had spent twenty years running from her roots.

"I don't know." Rob shook his blond head and glanced at her. "I've come to appreciate family more since I've been home. My dad is all I have now. I envy his relationship with your mom. They're starting over, and that's good for them."

"You sound awfully sentimental."

"Rose-colored glasses have a habit of obscuring my vision." He put a hand on her arm, his touch fueling a flame between them. "I see kids at the club from broken homes or dysfunctional families. I wish I could do something for them."

Kelly fought her natural flight mechanism. He must have noticed her uncomfortable bearing and the slight lift of her chin. He removed his hand slowly.

It was time to get away. Rob was too near and too big and too darn alive with his emotions exposed. She didn't want to feel the dangerous pull toward him. What happened to her earlier sense of self-control? She slurped down another swallow of lemonade, almost choking when a firecracker popped somewhere in the neighborhood. The whooshing sound of a bottle rocket followed.

"The kids are starting early," Rob said. He stood up and walked to the edge of the porch, looking down the street toward the square.

It was July Fourth. Independence Day. Kelly didn't feel independent. She felt tied to the past and to her insecurities. She stared at Rob's tall, strapping body, hardly believing he was standing there on her mother's porch. That she was there with him. After all these years.

He turned. "Have dinner with me tomorrow. Seven o'clock."

Kelly opened her mouth to say no, but the word stuck in her throat.

Rob rushed on. "I have to work tomorrow, of course, but I want to take you to the Tex-Mex restaurant on the square. I like to patronize local establishments. It's good for Heritage Springs' economy."

Kelly shut her mouth. Their gazes connected and held a brief moment. She was the first to look away.

"I'd like to get to know you better, Kel. Away from our parents. What do you say?"

She could do this. She was strong enough to keep her emotions in check. After all, she had done it for over twenty years.

"I guess so," she said as she lifted her gaze and caught speculation in Rob's eyes.

CHAPTER SEVEN

Monday morning

Practicality set in on Monday, that and a rising sense of panic skating through her midsection. Kelly left Heritage Springs and drove to Louisville, wishing she could keep on going. She excused her escape on the fact that she needed suitable clothing for her mother's wedding and for her date tonight.

Had she actually agreed to have dinner with Rob?

"Sure, Mom, you can stop by," C.B. said when Kelly called to tell her she was coming. "I'll be at work, but you have a key."

"There's good news about Aunt Bess's house," Kelly reported to her daughter. "The agent told me a young couple is coming back today for a second look."

"Great news! Fingers crossed."

"Yes, fingers crossed." Maybe she'd soon be free of one more obligation.

Fighting a sense of disconnect, Kelly drove across the county line. Driving into Louisville was not like coming home. How could it be? She no longer had a home.

Before leaving for Heritage Springs, Kelly had put her furniture and household items into storage and turned over the keys to her apartment. She had left extra clothing at her daughter's house— the daughter who was now married and no longer needed her.

Get a grip. She clutched the steering wheel. This whole creating a new life thing was being forced upon her whether she wanted it or not. She'd been through tough times before and survived. Surely she could manage this major redirection of her life.

I'm not going to wimp out.

C.B. and Daniel's home was a cute, red brick ranch in an established subdivision. C.B. had planted orange zinnias in large clay pots and placed them on her front stoop, providing a cheerful splash of color to welcome Kelly.

Tackling her bittersweet emotions, Kelly let herself into the house. The front door opened directly into the living room. Touches of C.B.'s personality were on display in the décor. Kelly liked the way a stuffed, chocolate-color sofa with plump beige throw pillows and a cozy easy chair, the oak drop-leaf table from Aunt Bess's house draped in a red and beige paisley runner and topped with framed photographs of horse shows, and a woven area rug that had the look of an Aubusson antique covering the hardwood floor played off each other.

The house was as neat as a pin too. What happened to that messy child who refused to clean up her bedroom? Kelly stood in the middle of the living room floor, her heart aching for that little girl. Bright sunshine sparkled through a picture window highlighting the swirls of red, green and beige in the area rug. A faint scent of cinnamon clung to the air, probably from the candles on the coffee table.

Kelly walked toward the fireplace and stared at a framed photograph on the mantle of C.B. and Daniel on their wedding day.

My little girl has grown up.

Inhaling a deep breath, Kelly surveyed the second framed photo, also from the wedding, of couple and their immediate families. Flanking Daniel were his two parents and three sisters with their spouses and a varied assortment of nieces and nephews. Only her mother and Kelly stood beside C.B.

The contrast was stark.

Kelly swallowed the lump in her throat along with another double dose of regret.

Pull yourself together!

Kelly tamped down the pang of guilt swirling in her head and went into the guest room. Opening the closet, she sorted through her clothes, scraping the hangers along the wooden rod. Nothing really worked. She would stop by Macy's before going back to Heritage Springs and find something that didn't make her look like a dowdy schoolmarm.

Stop it! Stop feeling sorry for yourself!

Children married and left home. Parents got on with their lives, even if they didn't have a life to get on with. What about Rob? He'd missed out on so many things in C.B.'s life, and he didn't even know it. Decisions long ago affected so many lives today—especially now that Rob had appeared again, as if out of the blue, and wanted to get to know her again. Ironic, wasn't it?

There was danger in tonight. Getting to know Rob again was not a smart idea. She could never tell him the truth. There would always be this secret between them—a secret he didn't know existed.

Right or wrong, she'd made her choices long ago. Rob would probably never forgive her if he found out about C.B.

Deep down a niggling fear caused her heart to ache as if a heavy hand had closed around it. Kelly paused in the living room to take another look around. Her daughter had created a comfortable home for herself and her husband. There was a sense of family here, of hope for the future. Of love. Despite her own feeling of inadequacy, she was truly happy for C.B. She and Aunt Bess had raised her right. That was something to congratulate herself about. Wasn't it? So why did the fear remain?

Her throat closed. What if, after learning the truth, C.B. never forgave her?

AWESOME! Kelly was absolutely awesome. Rob looked her up and down when she came to the door, his stomach muscles tightening as if he'd been punched.

"What?"

She was self-conscious. It amused him. And that touch of shyness coupled with her quick temper sparked his interest. Jessica would never have responded that way. He mentally shrugged. Maybe that was the trouble with their relationship, his ex-wife's lack of humility and disinterest. He would take Kelly's hostility any day compared to his wife's indifference.

"That blouse is really nice," he said, complimenting the relaxed, black and white tunic she wore over tight-fitting jeans. It fell below her slim hips and had a tantalizing scooped neckline. Jess had taught him about fashion, that and unfaithfulness.

"It's new." She shrugged off the flattery with a toss of her head and came out of the house, pulling the door shut.

How could she not know how beautiful she was?

They walked to the street, and he saw her eyeing his Beemer parked at the curb. "I thought we'd walk to the square," he said. "It's not far, and it's a nice evening."

Another shrug. "Sure, why not?"

He politely touched the small of her back through the black and white blouse as they walked away from the house. His pulse surged. Was it corny to admit his fingers tingled from the touch and that he was acutely, physically aware of her? She smelled like a field of flowers, her essence warm and romantic. Her hair, the color of copper, glinted with sun, and her body rippled with athletic grace as she walked.

Pure, raw sexual attraction, the first he felt since his divorce, drew him toward her. God, this was good and getting better each time he was with her. How had he forgotten this feeling of excitement? Like the time he was seventeen and hiding the fact a shy, homely girl gave him a hard-on?

A block before the square, he turned to her. "I wish I'd had the guts to openly ask you out years ago," he said.

She glanced askance but kept walking. "You know that wasn't possible."

"Your old man would have gone ballistic," he agreed.

"To say the least."

"Yet I wonder what would have happened, if I had mustered up the guts."

Kelly stopped, her gaze fastened on his face. She trained her features into a blank mask. "That wasn't possible. You and I were from different backgrounds. You had a college scholarship to look forward to."

A muscle worked in his jaw as he considered her view of things. "Strange, isn't it, that our parents have overcome the so-called differences in their backgrounds," he said quietly. "My guess is social class didn't matter as much as you thought."

Her eyes hardened. "I got knocked up. You had no business with someone like me."

A swift jab of jealousy hit him. "What was he like, your daughter's father?"

Kelly's shoulders stiffened, and she lifted her chin a determined notch. "Why bring this up?"

"Curiosity."

"What's done is done. It's history. You and I can never go back."

"Maybe we can go forward."

"Look, I agreed to dinner. Nothing more. Don't we have reservations?" Kelly turned on her heel and stalked away.

Rob caught up and lightly caught her left elbow where the balloon sleeve gathered. It was a gentleman's touch, but it connected them together whether Kelly wanted it or not.

DINNER TURNED out to be fun. Odd how a couple of margaritas could loosen up even the most reluctant dinner partner, Rob thought, and more than once hid a wicked smile. They devoured corn chips and hot salsa and then took on fat beef and bean burritos drenched in red enchilada sauce.

The key to Kelly opening up, besides the margaritas, was asking her about her daughter. Rob discovered C.B. had been a communications major at the University of Louisville and worked in an entry-level job for a healthcare insurance company. Her husband Daniel was in med school at the University of Louisville. C.B. had ridden Saddlebred horses as a child, but they could never afford to own one. Daniel was scared of horses, although he wanted to get a dog someday.

"Do you ride too?" Rob asked, liking the half-shy look in her eyes that gazed up at him under bronze eyelashes.

"I didn't want to live my life through my daughter." There was a tremor of satisfaction in her voice. "I took lessons too. It was fun."

Rob sat forward, intrigued. "Come with me Wednesday afternoon. I want to show you a project I've been working on for the children's club. It involves horses."

Kelly cocked her head, her gaze never leaving his. "Another date?"

"No, although another date wouldn't be a bad idea." He shrugged. "Come dressed to ride. We might be able to."

She placed an elbow on the table and rested her chin on her hand. "I suppose anything is better than being bored at my mother's."

He smiled with amusement. "That bad, huh?"

Kelly nodded, and continued resting her chin on the back of her hand, regarding him skeptically. "That bad."

They were quiet a minute, both concentrating on each other across the table. Kelly sat back and reached for her drink.

"What does C.B. stand for?" Rob asked.

"Colleen Baron," she replied and took a sip gazing at him over the rim of the stemmed glass.

"Colleen is a pretty name, but you shortened it to C.B."

"I've called her C.B. all her life."

He didn't ask why. Instead he studied her.

She crinkled her nose at him and placed her drink on the table. "You're staring again."

"I like to stare at you. You're good eye-candy," he said teasing.

"And you've become a pain in my side."

"No place else?"

"I was being polite," she came back.

"At least, I mean something to you."

Kelly crossed her arms defensively. "Don't count on it."

Mary Beth Jameson chose that moment to show up followed by her two teenage sons and ex-football player husband. They followed the hostess to a table, passing Kelly and Rob on the way to the back of the restaurant. Rob nodded. "Brett," he said, acknowledging the non-verbal greeting from Mary Beth's husband.

Of course, the woman stopped to chat. "Why, if it isn't Kelly Baron and Rob Scott," she exclaimed, her voice pitched high. "Fancy meeting you here." She winked at Kelly.

"Hello, Mary Beth," Kelly said.

"How are you?" Rob asked his high school classmate. He noted Kelly's stiff posture. Was she embarrassed being here with him?

"Are you two out on a date?" Mary Beth asked, her eyes wide with curiosity.

Kelly's eyes were smoldering. "We're just having dinner."

Mary Beth winked again. "Catching up on old times?"

Kelly looked as if she was gritting her teeth or at least biting her tongue. Rob spoke up to break the tension, "We're discussing our parents' upcoming wedding."

"I'm so sorry they're not having a big wedding," Mary Beth commented. "But given their age, I'm sure a private family ceremony will be just the right thing."

"Yes, we think so," Rob remarked dryly.

"Well, I see Brett waving. Got to go." Mary Beth bent low over the table and in a theatrical whisper said, "You make a cute couple."

Kelly waited until Mary Beth was seated and then said between clenched teeth, "That woman gets on my nerves."

Rob chuckled. "Ah, the disadvantages of a small town. Jessica could never quite accommodate herself to it." He sat back preferring to observe Kelly's reaction than to worry about the gossip Mary Beth was sure to stir up.

Kelly eyed her nearly empty glass. "Why did you bring Jessica to Heritage Springs?"

She lifted the glass to her lips and took a sip. Why was that motion sexy when Kelly did it? He swallowed hard, trying to douse his sudden need to taste those lips. To lick them dry of salt and lime. For a moment, he envied that margarita glass.

Rob shook himself mentally, trying to refocus. "I was tired of Chicago," he said. "The crowds, the trains, the politics. I even came to hate the rivalry between the Cubs and the White Sox."

"Why Heritage Springs though?" She cocked her head. "Why not live in a small city, such as Louisville?"

He glanced away, feeling her probing gaze. "Would you believe it if I told you I was homesick?" He turned and met her eyes once more.

"No." She paused thoughtfully. "But I've never been homesick. I never wanted to come home."

"I felt out of my league in Chicago." He paused. Kelly was the first person he had ever revealed that to. "I had a successful law firm, an expensive house in Highland Park, a happy marriage, so I thought, but at heart I remained a small town boy from Kentucky."

"You seem happy here."

"Happy enough." Rob lifted his hand for the waitress to bring the bill.

Kelly drained the last of her drink, wiped her mouth, and placed her rumpled napkin on the table.

"Good thing you're not driving," he quipped.

"You're assuming I can walk?"

He laughed and pushed his chair back to watch Kelly's face blush pink. "You're good for me, Kelly Baron," he said. "Thanks for coming back to town."

They strolled in silence up the hill to Kelly's house. He held her elbow as if to steady her perfectly steady gait. She didn't pull away. *Why?*

He wondered about many things, especially her much beloved daughter C.B. He wanted to ask Kelly more about the grown girl. He was cautious. What happened in Kelly's past was none of his business. Apparently, she hadn't been the nun most guys had thought. He knew about one time. Must have been more times with other guys.

All he knew was that he liked the grownup Kelly and didn't want the night to end. "Care to sit on the swing?"

"No, I'd better go in."

"Curfew?"

"No." She turned at the door and stared at him. A tiny smile curved her lips.

"Scared?"

Her smile faded. "Yes."

A rising swell of desire flooded through his body. He wanted her.

Rob touched her upper arms lightly. "Of me?"

"Of many things. Myself, especially."

"Then I'll say good night." He didn't want to push her. She looked as if she were a filly about to break and run.

Very carefully Rob reached up and tenderly touched Kelly's cheek with a fingertip, leaving a symbolic kiss and the promise of more to come.

CHAPTER EIGHT

Tuesday morning

Today I'm forty.

Kelly tried to ignore the fact as she stared at herself in the bath-room mirror the next morning and plucked a gray hair from the top of her head. For some reason being forty seemed so *old*. Yet she felt the same, and as Rachel kept reminding her, she had her whole life ahead of her.

Kelly could no longer ignore the inevitable when she entered her mother's sparse kitchen ten minutes later and discovered a colorful, wrapped birthday gift setting on the table.

She paused. The aroma of brewing coffee filled the room. A clock ticked on the wall. Kelly slowly lifted the small, flat box and stared at it. Decorated in pink and purple paper with a purple bow on top, the box looked professionally wrapped. Something about it said *expensive*.

Her mother came in. "Open it," she urged.

Kelly glanced up. "You didn't have to buy me a gift. I've been trying to avoid this day."

"I wanted to get you something. Something special. You're my daughter."

Smiling slightly, Kelly fought back a strange sadness. When had her mother made such a big deal out of her birthday? In the past, when controlled by her strict husband, her mother didn't make this day special. What was different this year? Her father was gone, of course, and Howie was in the picture. Maybe that was it.

Kelly's throat tightened and she slipped the tape from the end of the package with a fingernail, peeling off the paper. She lifted the lid. On a cushion of cotton rested a pair of diamond teardrop earrings.

"They're fourteen karat white gold," her mother said, apprehension in her voice.

Kelly glanced up to meet the nervousness in her mother's eyes. She so wanted to please. "You shouldn't have done this," she said, shaking her head. "You don't have this kind of money, Mother."

"Howie helped me pick them out and pay for them."

Was this in reality a gift from her soon-to-be stepfather? A way to buy her consent to this whole miserable affair? Kelly didn't want these flashy earrings any more than she wanted to be here. Unfortunately, she had to accept them. If she turned the gift down, she would hurt her mother's feelings. Kelly didn't want to do that. She loved her mother.

Looking down, Kelly picked an earring from the box and held it up, meeting her mother's eyes again. "They're lovely. Thank you."

"Do you really like them?" Her mother hovered near, almost wringing her hands in relief. "I was so afraid you wouldn't. Maybe you can wear them to the wedding."

"Yes, maybe I can."

With a heavy heart, Kelly slowly inserted the stud into her earlobe. The earring was light. It tickled her cheek when she moved her head. She picked up the other earring and inserted it. Her mother's eyes were alight with pleasure.

"What do you think?" Kelly cocked her head to one side and smiled.

"They're beautiful. You're beautiful. I love you so much."

"I love you too, Mother. Thank you."

Her mother hesitated. Then she took a step forward and hugged Kelly.

Why couldn't you have done this when I really needed it?

Kelly shut her eyes and returned the hug, sorrow overwhelming her.

LATER IN HER ROOM, Kelly finished packing away all of the old items she didn't want. She stripped the pink and purple flowered bedspread from the Jenny Lind bed leaving only the sheets and the blanket and packed them into a box to donate, probably to Rob's yard sale. The bed was perfect for C.B.'s new house. Kelly's heart warmed as she envisioned it in a child's bedroom.

With the drawers empty and the old clothes in the closet packed away, only the Cabbage Patch doll skipped the donation pile. It sat forlornly on the bed by itself.

As she stood in the middle of the room surveying the footlocker, which she still needed to address, Kelly's iPhone played a "Danny Boy" ringtone. She picked it up from the dresser. "Hi, C.B."

"Happy birthday, Mom!"

"Thank you." Kelly couldn't keep the grin from her voice. She loved hearing from her daughter.

"I'm sorry Daniel and I can't make it up there today, but we'll see you Friday night and bring our gift then."

"I understand." Kelly sat down on the bed. "I'm trying to ignore my birthday anyway."

"Ah, Mom."

Kelly changed the subject quickly. "Would you like my old Jenny Lind bed for your guest room? I can have it moved."

They talked a minute about the bed and her mother's plans for the house. Kelly didn't mention Rachel's idea. Staying in Heritage Springs and running a bed and breakfast was a non-starter as far as she was concerned. Yet she still didn't have any plans for what she'd do after Friday night's wedding. She refused to think that far.

"Mom?"

C.B.'s voice was full of indecision. "What, pumpkin?"

"There's a girl at work who recently found her birth father," C.B. said out of the blue.

"That's nice." Kelly kept her tone noncommittal.

C.B. took a breath. "Turns out her father is a recovering drug addict, not the man she imagined."

Kelly said nothing, unable to speak.

"It's really sad for my friend," C.B. went on quickly, her voice sounding troubled.

"I bet it is," Kelly finally replied, swallowing her fear. "Why do you bring this up?"

"I was wondering about my own father."

Kelly clenched the iPhone. "We talked about him when you were a teenager and agreed it was better for you not to know anything about him."

"Yes, Mom, but that was before I married Daniel." C.B.'s voice grew bolder. "He says we need to know my family history for when we have children. Suppose I'm a carrier of some sort of genetic disease. It would make a difference whether we decide to have children or not."

Kelly's heart contracted with pain, forming a hard knot in her chest. The day she dreaded had arrived. "You can trust me when I say you'll be okay to have children."

"That's not the point, Mom." C.B. raised her voice. "Daniel says unless you don't know who my father is, you should tell me. He says I have the right to know."

When had Daniel taken over? If Kelly wouldn't name C.B.'s father, was Daniel implying she'd been a slut? Kelly gritted her teeth, biting back sudden anger. C.B. was her child. She knew what was best, and keeping the secret of her father had never interfered with their relationship until now. Until Daniel.

"Daniel doesn't have anything to say about this."

"He's my husband," C.B. said simply.

Tears burned behind Kelly's eyes. She controlled her voice and spoke softly, "He may be, but I'm still your mother. I know what's best."

"Do you, Mom?" C.B. cried. "Do you?"

"I don't want you to get hurt."

"You can't protect me forever. I have the right to know my family history."

Kelly heard the determination in her daughter's voice. "We'll talk about this later,"

"Sure, Mom. Later, always later. When are you going to stop running?"

The conversation came to an abrupt end when the phone went dead. Kelly slowly lowered her iPhone and clutched it in her right hand. She stared straight ahead at the faded, bare wall.

What am I going to do?

Nothing at the moment. She would coast along as always, avoiding the hard stuff and doing her best.

THAT EVENING KELLY and her mother dined at Howie's house, a spectacular custom-built home in the Locust Grove subdivision and the expensive part of town. The three-story Victorian, finished seven years earlier, had gray siding and a wrap-around porch.

At their knock Howie opened the door wide, stepping back to let them enter his home. "Welcome!"

Mother is going to live here? Kelly's first impression of the interior was one of awe and delight. A wide cherry staircase swept from the second floor to the dark hardwood of the open foyer.

"Isn't it lovely?" her mother asked when she noticed Kelly eyeing the grand staircase.

"Perfect for a lovely bride," Howie interrupted proudly before Kelly answered.

"Oh, Howie, you're so sweet." Her mother grasped his outstretched hand, and Howie pulled her into a loving embrace.

To escape, Kelly turned quickly and entered the living room with its warming buttery yellow walls. The floor-to-ceiling windows were dressed with plantation shutters and accented with drawn-back, burnt-orange drapes.

"Are they at it again?"

She stopped at the sound of the very familiar male voice. Rob rose from a wingback chair, glass in hand, and grinned at her with a flash of appreciation in his eyes.

"Public display of affection," Kelly told him. "You said I'd get used to it, but I seriously doubt it."

He laughed, dismissing her concern. "Can I get you something to drink?"

"No thank you."

"Come on. A little wine? Another margarita?"

"No!"

He laughed again as if they shared a secret.

Kelly stood awkwardly in the wide doorway staring at C.B.'s father. Guilt washed over her. Guilt and fear. "Okay, maybe a little wine. Something red."

"My pleasure." Rob went to the sidebar as their parents came into the room, arms wrapped around each other's waist.

"Have a seat, Kelly." Howie escorted her mother to an ivory sofa. "Do you want something to drink, dear?"

"Nothing, darling."

Darling? Kelly mentally rolled her eyes as her gaze traveled between her mother and Howie, who sat down beside her and picked up his martini glass from the coffee table. A jar of faux lemons and a silk floral arrangement brightened the cherry coffee table.

"This is an Australian Shiraz." Rob returned and handed Kelly a wine glass. "It's a fruity variety. I hope you like it sweet."

"I'm sure it will be fine." As she took the glass, Kelly gazed up into the blue depths of Rob's eyes, fighting the painful lump in her throat.

"Take my chair," Rob offered. He brought a dining room chair into the room and sat down, watching Kelly over the rim of his glass.

Kelly watched him back, afraid to speak, her heart thudding in her throat. A rope of memories connected them as they sat there staring at each other across the room.

C.B. wanted to know about her father. How could she tell her daughter the truth after keeping the secret for so many years? If C.B. found out her father was a perfectly respectable lawyer, would she ever understand Kelly's reasoning—the pure panic of finding out she was pregnant, the fear of her father and for the safety of her unborn child, Mrs. Scott's interference, and the lack of support from anyone but Aunt Bess who urged her to move away from Heritage Springs?

No. C.B. would never understand. Kelly hardly understood herself any more.

Full of black despair, Kelly scowled, looking away, unable to meet Rob's eyes any longer.

This was not going to be a good evening.

AT THE URGING of their parents, Rob left the dinner table to show Kelly the garden. Kelly's last image as she left the house was of Howie and her mother sitting in the living room where her mother was pouring coffee from a silver coffee pot into dainty Wedgewood cups. Her mother looked happy, at ease in her new environment. She handled the three-piece silver coffee service as if she had been born to do it

Kelly battled against a sick feeling that rose in her throat. When had her world turned upside down? Everything was skewed, especially her feelings.

"We were set up again," Rob said strolling beside her, his faded jeans hugging his long legs and lean hips.

"I'm sorry about that." Kelly felt her face warm as Rob surveyed her quietly.

"I don't mind. Your mother is persistent."

"Is that how she snagged your father?"

Rob shook his head. "No, I think it was more like shared circumstances and loneliness. My father had two good marriages. After his second wife died, he didn't like living alone."

Heart hammering, Kelly glanced away. "I suppose you can get used to it. What about you? Do you like living alone?"

Leaves rustled in a gentle summer breeze. A wide walkway of cool, gray stones led around a carefully pruned magnolia tree. A blue-gray wooden fence provided privacy, shutting them off from the windows in the back of the house. Green shrubs and colorful perennials were confined to well-manicured beds flanked by softball-sized white rocks.

Rob ran his fingers through his hair. "I've never gotten used to living alone. You probably have no problem with it."

She met his gaze once more. "No. I've always lived with my daughter or Aunt Bess."

They walked a few more steps. "Any boyfriends?" he challenged her. "Or do forty-year-old women call the men they date 'boyfriends'?"

"Oh, cute." Kelly scoffed. "Did my mother tell you it's my birthday?"

Rob watched her closely. "She didn't have to," he said. "We went to school together, remember?" He made a soft sound of amusement. "You didn't answer me about your boyfriends."

"I've had my share over the years," she hedged. His stare was making her uneasy.

"Nothing serious?"

"No. What about you? Or are you gun-shy after your divorce?" she asked, hoping to focus his attention in another direction.

Rob lifted an eyebrow "Ah, so we change the subject." They walked on without speaking further until they came to a weathered, wooden bench. A water feature bubbled nearby, the water flowing over gray stones into a small, dark pond also surrounded by softball-sized rocks.

Rob sat on the bench, and Kelly sat beside him, inwardly shrinking from his oh-so-tempting nearness.

"Why do you want to know?" he asked, continuing the train of conversation.

"Just curious."

"Because you care about me?"

Her heart plummeted. How did she answer that question? *Did* she care about him? Or were the rising pulses and shallow breathing a throwback to what happened between them long ago?

"If you don't want to talk about it, I understand. It's really none of my business." She avoided his question quite deftly.

As if he read her thoughts, Rob shook his head. "I don't mind telling you about it." He rested against the back of the bench and stretched out his legs. His jaw flexed. "I was the last one to know."

Kelly didn't miss the bridled anger in his voice. "Know what?"

"That my wife was having an affair."

The silence between them was heavy.

"Isn't that the way it always is?" Kelly said feeling his pain. Hadn't she dodged entanglements trying to avoid the hurt Rob had experienced?

He nodded again. "I suppose the wronged spouse wears rose-colored glasses until it's too late."

Uncomfortable, Kelly tried to back off. "You really don't have to tell me."

Rob sat forward and clasped his hands. "I want to, *if* you don't mind listening."

The weird reality of sitting there with Rob made her pulse rate soar. Kelly felt vulnerable. Out of control. She had trained herself well, but to no avail today.

"I don't mind," she heard a voice that sounded like hers say.

With a slight scowl on his face, Rob twisted around to face her. "I met Jessica in law school and fell in love. We had fun. We laughed. We worked and played hard. Our wedding was a big, fancy occasion with two hundred guests. I started my own firm while she worked in a large one. After ten years, we tried to have a child. Jessica miscarried."

Rob's clipped explanation stopped abruptly. It took him a minute to regain his composure. Kelly watched the play of sadness and anger on his face.

Then he went on more softly. "Our relationship was different after that. We didn't have sex for several months and then only sporadically. She worked long hours. I wanted to have children, but Jessica said she didn't. 'She was finished abusing her body,' she said." Rob paused. Unspoken pain intensified in his eyes. "I thought moving to Heritage Springs would do us good. A year and a half ago, I found out she was sleeping with a lawyer from her old firm." He scraped fingers through his hair. "Our marriage was over."

"Wow," Kelly whispered unable to think of anything more appropriate to say. Her heart bled for him. What a hard break—to have it all and then lose everything.

Rob gave her a half-hearted smile as if trying to pull himself together. "What happened to me is nothing unusual. Many wives cheat on their husbands."

"But it happened to *you*, not someone else. Of course you're hurt." Kelly experienced a gut-deep anger, reacting the way she knew she'd feel herself.

"I don't know why I told you this," he said in a controlled voice. "We haven't seen each other in years."

Kelly shrugged unsure of what to say. Suddenly she didn't want to share his confidences or his sorrow. She didn't want to care about him.

"Maybe it's because of your daughter."

"What do you mean?" Her stomach tightened as her preservation instinct kicked in.

"Because you have your own child," he murmured. "I thought you would understand how important it is for me to have a child of my own. I always wanted to be a father."

Swallowing hard, Kelly was unable to meet his gaze. The secret she held in her heart sizzled, making her suddenly even more vulnerable to the miserable look in his eyes.

"You never married," he continued. "I guess that's why I wanted to tell you. I thought you'd understand because some S.O.B. must have hurt you once."

Torn by conflicting emotions, Kelly shifted to face him. "Yes," she said. "Some son of a bitch hurt me like hell."

CHAPTER NINE

Wednesday afternoon

He wanted to be a father. Admitting that to Kelly focused the root of his sadness as nothing else in the past three years had done. The next day Rob left the courthouse, walking briskly down the steps to the square and around the sidewalk to his office in an old building on the right corner of the square.

His secretary Gail greeted him cheerily when he arrived. "You have a guest waiting in your office."

He opened the door to his office. *Kelly.*

She stood with her back to the door surveying his rows of law books in a floor-to-ceiling bookshelf behind his desk. She wore denim full-length riding pants with long suede patches inside the calves. The jodhpurs fit her close from the waist to the ankle ending with flared bell-bottoms. She had tucked a pale blue chambray shirt into the waistband and rolled up her long sleeves.

Kelly was sexy. One hundred percent. Every fiber of his being revved with excitement.

A powerful rush of desire filled his veins. He turned and grinned back at Gail without embarrassment. "Thanks," he said, knowing now why she had given him that saucy wink.

Kelly turned and caught him staring. "What?"

"I like the way you look since you've grown up."

Blushing delicately, she stepped around his desk to confront him eye-to-eye, as if challenging him to say more. "Have you read all those books?" she asked instead.

"Not even half," he said with a short laugh. Circling the desk, he placed his brief case on the top but didn't open it. "You must remember this was my father's office. Many of them are his."

"Oh, that's right."

She stood ill at ease, shifting her stance and staring at him. Red hair framed her oval face. Kelly's milk-white complexion was tanned from summer sun. What did she like to do? Did she read books and knit? He didn't know much about her, but was anxious to learn.

"I see you came ready to ride."

She followed his gaze as he gave her an approving up and down once over. Her body stiffened in defense. "I thought you told me to."

"I did." He grinned, enjoying her discomfiture. "Let me change my clothes, and we'll get going."

ROB DIDN'T HAVE fancy jodhpurs, only regular blue jeans. He did wear a pair of waterproof, lace-up paddock boots, which were perfect for trips to the barn and his infrequent horseback rides.

"We have to pick up the kids first," Rob told Kelly as he handed her into his maroon Honda Ridgeline. No BMW for him today.

"I never figured you as a truck sort of guy."

Good, he had surprised her. "Maybe you don't know me very well," he teased.

She settled into the front of the cab and buckled up. "Apparently."

Rob drove a couple of blocks from the square and stopped in front of the Heritage Springs Children's Club, a refurbished hardware store that now housed the local charity organization. Thanks to the Rotary Club, part of the parking lot had been fenced off to create a well-used playground that was currently crawling with shouting children.

"Wait here. I won't take long."

"Sure."

The sisters Tara and Courtney were waiting for him at the door. He signed them out, as always on Wednesdays, and walked hand-and-hand with them to the truck. They scrambled into the back seat, and Rob made sure they buckled up.

"Tara and Courtney, this is Miss Baron. She's going riding with us today."

Kelly turned and looked over the seat, smiling. "Hi," she said. "But please call me Kelly."

"Hi, Kelly," Tara said. "Do you like horses too?"

"I love them." Kelly's face was bright. "Which one are you?"

"I'm Tara. Courtney's shy."

Kelly nodded. "I'm shy too, Courtney. It's okay. Do you like horses?"

The smaller child nodded her head. "Yes, ma'am."

Rob climbed in the front and started the engine. "I help the girls' mother pay for riding lessons," he explained as he pulled onto the street. "It's our Wednesday thing together, isn't it girls?"

"Yes, Rob," the two chimed in together.

Rob glanced sideways at Kelly, then back to the road. *Good.* He could almost see Kelly's mind whirling. He had surprised her once more and he liked that. Surprising her was part of his plan.

Knowing the high price of falling in love didn't stop him. Maybe he liked wearing rose-colored glasses. The world looked better to him with them on.

THIS IS FOLLY, Kelly chided herself silently watching Rob help Tara and Courtney out of the truck. Then the girls raced ahead of them toward the barn, which was a long metal structure located two miles outside of town. The sign on the road by the entrance had read *Pat's Riding Academy and Stables.* The facility looked well maintained with its surrounding pastures fenced by dark creosote posts and rails.

"Bet you didn't know we have a saddle seat instructor in town now."

Kelly glanced up at Rob to see the twinkle in his eyes. Did he enjoy surprising her? "No, I didn't."

"Pat received a nice settlement in her divorce and decided to move from the northern Chicago area and set up her barn," he explained.

The gravel crunched beneath her feet. Kelly cocked her head to get a better look at the man who raised an eyebrow in amusement.

"Why do I get the feeling you had something to do with this?" She swept her arm out toward the barn and pastureland.

"Psychic?"

"Not a chance."

He shrugged, not hiding a telltale grin. "I'm a good lawyer, and Pat liked my relocation suggestion."

Kelly felt her cheeks flush warmly at the way he stared at her. If he didn't quit looking at her like that, she'd... She would do what? Kiss him? The impulse played havoc with her mind, and she strode faster, as if she could avoid him.

She couldn't, of course. He caught up with her quickly enough, and they passed through the wide-open doorway of the barn.

Inside the dark aisles flanked by stalls full of curious horses poking their noses up against the bars, Kelly's body relaxed. The familiar smells of horseflesh, leather, and cedar shavings filled her with a quiet calmness. Why had she stopped riding? It was such a mind-clearer, a way to release tension. A thirty-minute lesson aboard a spirited American Saddlebred horse did more for her well being than anything else she had ever found.

They followed the sounds of excited little girls to two stalls at the end of the aisle. Standing with Tara and Courtney in a stall with a small spotted pony was a trim, gray-haired woman dressed in Kentucky jochpurs, paddock boots, and a green T-shirt.

At their approach, she turned welcoming them with a smile. "Your girls are beside themselves as usual, Rob."

Rob laughed warmheartedly. "Pat, this is my friend Kelly. I asked her to tag along with us today."

Pat stepped to the door of the stall and stuck out her hand. "Glad to meet you."

Kelly grabbed the calloused hand. Pat's grip was firm as if she had all the confidence in the world. "Good to meet you too."

"I see you ride," Pat said, marking the way Kelly was dressed.

"Yes, I've taken a few lessons. Saddle seat."

"Terrific. I guess Rob told you we're a saddle seat barn."

"Yes, he mentioned it." Although saddle seat was an English style of riding, it was uniquely American having originated on the plantations of the Confederate South and developed to show off elegant, easy-riding pleasure horses.

Further conversation was put on hold because of the anxious little girls, hopping from one foot to the other, eager to ride.

And ride they did. Kelly and Rob watched them from the middle of a large indoor arena covered with a floor of dirt and sawdust. Little Courtney rode an easy-going black and white pony named Cookie while Tara was aboard a retired Saddlebred show horse nicknamed Spook.

"Shorten your snaffle reins, Tara," Pat instructed as both children and mounts circled and circled the arena hugging the inside walls. "Courtney, heels down! Raise your hands."

From what Kelly could tell, Pat was an excellent instructor, patient and competent, but what interested her most was Rob's reaction to the lessons. The tenderness in his expression amazed her. His gaze never left the two girls as they completed their various gaits. When Tara was asked to canter, Kelly watched Rob's body language also urging the big bay horse into the gait. After a few stops and starts, Tara accomplished her task, and as the horse and rider cantered around the arena, Rob mouthed a happy "yes" and pumped his fist in triumph.

More uncertain than ever, Kelly stood quietly, her heart pounding, as Pat barked instructions and Rob followed the lessons with an intensity of any proud parent.

He would be a good father.

A wave of understanding washed over her as well as a heavy swell of guilt. Rob had a child—one he didn't know existed. Somehow her decision as a scared, pregnant teen was coming back to haunt her in the worst way. Had she made a terrible mistake? Should she have told Rob the truth back then, no matter the threat from his mother and her father? At eighteen, would he have stepped up and done the right thing by her?

All water over the dam, as the old adage went. Much too late to change the choices she made. If what she had done was a mistake, then she had to live with its consequences.

The secret in her heart formed a hard knot in her chest, and she knew she must keep it no matter what.

"It's a good thing what Rob does for those girls," Pat said to Kelly.

They watched from the door of the barn as Rob walked the two children to their mother's late model Chevy. A young woman in blue jeans came around the old car to greet them, and Kelly imagined the little girls were telling her all about their exciting lessons. Soon Rob knelt down and, one at a time, both girls hugged his neck, and then he stood and helped them climb into the car and buckle up.

"Their dad deserted the family and Bekah has struggled. She could never afford sixty dollars a week for lessons," Pat explained.

Kelly watched the scene unfolding in the distance with Rob's kindness and generosity on display. Why did it soften her heart? Fill her with regrets? She didn't want to react to him. After all, she'd be gone Saturday morning after the wedding and never have to see him again.

Drawing a quick breath at her naïveté, Kelly straightened her shoulders and stared ahead. Who was she kidding? Her mother was marrying his dad. She and Rob would be thrown together at family events from now on.

"Any chance we can take that trail ride?" Rob asked walking toward them with long strides, his powerful well-muscled body moving with ease.

"Sure thing," Pat answered. "All we have to do is put another saddle on Spook and tack Rival." She turned and headed into the barn.

Kelly looked up and met Rob's twinkling eyes. "Trail ride?"

"I thought it would be fun." He inclined his blond head. "If you're up to it."

"Are you challenging me?"

"Of course I am."

She couldn't resist him. The fondness and amusement in his blue eyes compelled her to say yes.

Kelly ducked her head as if avoiding her own self-destructive compulsion. She didn't understand why she wasn't running away this time. "Okay," she said, "I accept the challenge."

His face triumphant, Rob headed to the tack room and returned with two riding helmets. Placing one on a tack trunk, he lifted the other one high above her head, lowered it, and fitted it snuggly in place.

He was much too near. His towering presence overpowered her. She inhaled sharply at the contact of his fingers under her chin. Her gaze locked with his, and then she couldn't breathe, her heart pounding as if it was trying to escape her chest. A smoldering flame lit in his eyes. He slowly hooked the chinstrap.

Who knew the mere act of putting on a riding helmet could be so sexy? It was freaking her out.

But she wouldn't let him help her mount. The thought of having his hands touching anywhere on her body accelerated her already racing heart. She pressed her lips firmly together.

Pat led Rival out of the stall into the aisle and held his head while Kelly pulled up a sturdy plastic stepstool near to the bay horse's left side.

"Rob, hold Kelly's stirrup, will you?"

"I'd rather give her a leg-up." His voice carried a teasing quality, but his eyes spoke his serious intent.

"Not on your life!" Kelly stepped on the stool, gathered her reins, and with hands gripping the front and back of the saddle, stuck her boot into the left stirrup.

On the other side of the horse, Rob held her right stirrup to keep the saddle in place as her weight shifted it to the left. "At least I'm good for something," he quipped.

Kelly glared at him and swung into the saddle longing to just accidently kick him in his handsome face. But she resisted the impulse and settled into the saddle instead. Getting the feel of the leather beneath her, she picked up the double reins adjusting them between her fingers.

"You know what you're doing," Pat commented after observing her actions. "I won't worry about you."

The praise raised Kelly's spirits. Maybe she could survive the trail ride after all. Who knew, it might even be fun.

RIDING SPOOK out of the barn into the bright afternoon sunshine, Rob fought to control his high spirits. Did agreeing to the trail ride mean Kelly was slowly coming around? He had seen a spark of interest in her eyes and wanted to press his advantage.

Turning in the saddle, he placed a hand on the horse's rump and looked back at Kelly. She followed on Rival. He was another retired Saddlebred with a shiny chestnut coat. The helmet hid her red hair, but her coloring complemented that of the horse. She was relaxed in the saddle, as if born to ride. Her denim jodhpurs, extending longer than the heel of her boots in back and covering the arch of the foot, made her legs appear long and elegant.

He loved the look of her in the saddle. He loved the look of her all the time. Rob's heart warmed, and he knew he wanted more from Kelly than she was probably willing to give.

"The trail runs along the outside of Pat's pasture and goes down to the creek. Just follow me," he told her, deciding he'd do something about her reluctance.

"I wouldn't think of doing anything else." Her answer was glib.

He laughed as he turned around. Rob also loved her testiness. He loved her spunk. She might believe herself to be shy, but there was a steel quality underneath everything. How else had she survived the heartache life had thrown at her? God, he admired her for that.

They walked their horses along the back fencerow. Rob found the rhythm of the slow gait and the crunch of dry grass under the horses' hooves soothing. He relaxed in the saddle, always mindful of Kelly behind him keeping pace.

The trail led down to a lower pasture, following the outer fence. Inside the pasture, horses grazed. Overhead a black crow cawed from the top of a maple tree as if standing watch over them. Fifteen minutes into the ride the trail dipped toward the creek. Rob gave Spook his head going down the rocky embankment. Low from lack of rain, the creek made a lazy path winding its way along the back of Pat's property.

Stopping at the edge of the creek, Rob let Kelly and Rival catch up. They halted beside him. Kelly rested her hands on the pommel of the saddle.

"This is pretty," she said looking out across the shallow water.

"Not as pretty as you."

"Rob!"

"What? You don't like a compliment?"

"I don't like you pressing me," she replied as she set her jaw in anger.

"Pressing? I'm just stating the obvious." He turned Spook to the left and circled around, coming in alongside Rival so close that his knee brushed up against Kelly's thigh. "I've always thought you beautiful, Kelly."

She studied him a moment and then looked away.

With his left hand, Rob reached across his body and touched Kelly's chin. Gently he urged her to turn her head. When she did, he saw a mixture of anguish and longing in her eyes.

"I've missed you, Kelly."

She wet her lips. "What am I to say to that?"

"Don't say anything."

He cupped her chin and pulled her face toward him. Leaning nearer, he angled his head to the side and then covered her mouth with his. Her lips were warm and pliable. He devoured their softness, hungry for more, asking for more, not expecting anything.

Parting her lips, Kelly raised herself in the saddle, tilting toward him, and kissed him back.

CHAPTER TEN

Thursday morning

"I don't understand why you're so upset," Rachel said, her voice sounding as if it was next door even though it was coming through Kelly's iPhone.

"I kissed a man!"

Rachel laughed. "You should be doing more of that. What's wrong with this man?"

"He's not just any man," Kelly said. *No, he's C.B.'s father.* Her heart caved in her chest crushing her with fear and pain. "I…ah…dated him in high school," she went on to explain to her best friend.

"So?"

"So I shouldn't be kissing him!"

"Is he married?"

"Divorced."

"Then what's the problem?" Rachel's question hung between them like a heavy obstacle. "Oh, I get it. You enjoyed it!"

Kelly licked her lips. God help her. She *had* enjoyed it.

"Kelly?"

"Yes." Her response was a bit too sharp.

"Are you falling for this guy?"

"No!" She couldn't. Wouldn't. What was happening to her?

"Take a deep breath, sweetie. You don't have to marry this man just because you enjoyed kissing him."

Kelly sunk onto her mattress, putting the death grip on her iPhone. Her stripped bedroom felt cold and impersonal, as if ghosts of childhood past were haunting the room. "You're right," she said, inhaling deeply. "It's just one kiss."

"Then why are you upset?"

Because he may find out the truth and hate me.

When she didn't speak up, Rachel pressured her again. "You dated milquetoast Thomas so long you've forgotten how a real, hot-blooded man behaves. From what I gather, he likes you. Why not let this play out a little? See where it goes."

"Because I don't intend to stay in Heritage Springs," Kelly shot back. "I'm supposed to be finding myself, remember? I plan to head to Beaufort on Saturday to visit you."

"But suppose you *find* yourself in Heritage Springs? Suppose this guy is the one you're supposed to build your new life around?

"Because he isn't." Kelly was tired of the discussion. It was going nowhere. "If you don't want me to come, I'll change my plans."

"Of course I want you to come."

"I'll be there Sunday."

"Okay." Rachel paused. "But if you change your plans, all you have to do is call."

"I won't."

"Of course not."

She heard the grin in her friend's voice. "Good-bye, Rachel," Kelly said through gritted teeth.

"See you Sunday," Rachel answered. "Maybe."

Maybe? There was no maybe about it. She wasn't sticking around. It was too dangerous. Kelly had no intention of falling under Rob Scott's spell.

Irritated at herself, she forced down the knot of fear in her stomach. Then her gaze fell on the footlocker setting in the middle of the floor where Rob had dropped it. One last obligation to complete.

If I can find the key.

Kelly thought a minute trying to recall the last time she had shut the footlocker. Lying back on the bed, her hands behind her head, she stared at the ceiling for a long time, unwinding, breathing deeply, and trying to solve the mystery of the key.

Suddenly, she sat up and swung her legs over the side of the bed. Following a sixth sense, she stood up and walked to the dresser pulling open the bottom drawer. Reaching underneath it, her fingers touched the key taped to the bottom.

As she opened the footlocker, Kelly inhaled and then exhaled long and hard. She sat down cross-legged on the floor and peeked inside ready to toss the contents—a ragged stuffed bear, a stack of yellowed English composition papers with red "A's" emblazoned across them, and aged photographs showing the disaster she'd been in high school with her long-sleeve blouses, long skirts and long hair pinned up in an old-fashioned bun.

Yearbooks from all four years were there. Reluctant to relive unwanted memories, Kelly didn't open them. She shoved them aside and beneath them found a blue spiral-bound notebook.

My diary.

A cold chill ran through her chest. Slowly, Kelly removed the notebook and placed it in her lap. Staring at it, touching it, she fought the recurring anxiety this trip to Heritage Springs had ignited. In the end, curiosity overcame common sense. She opened the notebook.

Most of it was filled with anger at her father and the horrid restrictions he forced upon her. "Two boys made fun of me today in history class," she'd written twenty-two years ago. "They called me Amish girl and said I was ugly. I wouldn't let them see how their words hurt me. Rob was in the class. He didn't say anything to them, because we had an agreement we wouldn't talk in school, but I saw in his eyes how angry he was at them. I knew he wanted to defend me."

Kelly licked her lips, fighting back tears as the humiliation came back full force. She had hated high school. Heritage Springs. Her father. She had wanted to escape from this rotten, miserable little town. She didn't regret leaving.

Kelly set her jaw, knowing she had done the right thing.

On the last two pages of the notebook she discovered more. "Rob doesn't know," she had written in her scrawling handwriting. "I can't tell him. His mother may already suspect something. She warned me to stay away from him. I had to tell him we couldn't go together any more. I didn't tell him why. He told me I was breaking his heart."

Her head bowed, Kelly slumped in despair. Rob had cared about her so many years ago. Had she really broken his heart? She couldn't believe it. Didn't want to believe it. She'd done what she had to do to save their child. That was all. The bottom line. The end.

Kelly rose from the floor and ripped the pages from the notebook. She tore them in two again and again until she shredded them into strips of paper, destroying the evidence of that horrible, hurtful life.

CHAPTER ELEVEN

Howie's house
Thursday evening

Her mother was sobbing. Kelly stood helplessly in the living room of Howie's house watching her soon-to-be-stepfather envelop her mother into his arms, comforting her like a child.

"What's wrong?" Rob came into the room carrying two glasses of wine. He handed one to Kelly, looking about as awkward as she felt.

"She got a phone call and just started crying," Kelly said with a shrug. The fact that her stoic, always steady mother was having a major meltdown startled her. She had never before seen such a show of emotion from her mother.

Rob took a sip of wine, observing the scene with a lawyer's eye. "My guess is pre-wedding jitters."

"I suppose so."

Howie led Grace to the sofa. She sat down, and he gave her his clean handkerchief. Kelly hadn't seen a man with a white handkerchief in years, not since her father. She frowned at the comparison. From what she could tell, Howard Scott was one hundred percent more caring than her father had ever been.

"It seems there's a slight predicament," Howie told them, trying to hide his sympathetic grin.

"Anything we can do to help, Dad?"

"I'm not sure. It seems June Hobson broke her arm yesterday and is unable to bake the strawberry wedding cake."

Kelly rolled her eyes. Was that all?

"I had my heart set on a strawberry cake," Grace said sniffling. "Now we don't even have a wedding cake."

It wasn't the end of the world. The wedding party tomorrow was small—only a few relatives. Surely they could get by without a wedding cake.

"We'll make one," Rob said. His gaze bathed Kelly with half-concealed amusement, the corners of his eyes crinkling.

"What?"

"Kelly and I will go to the store and buy enough cake mix and icing to make you *two* cakes, Grace," Rob declared. "We won't let your wedding day be ruined for lack of a strawberry cake."

ROB WASN'T JOKING. An hour later Kelly walked through the front door of his home.

"I still don't understand why we have to bake the cake at your house." She heard the childish pout in her voice.

"Because your mother's kitchen is a mess and my dad's house is cleaned up for the wedding."

"Something makes me think there's more to it than that."

Hands clutching cloth grocery bags, Rob kicked the door shut. "I can't deny I wanted to get you alone."

Kelly was unprepared for the giddy heat that raced through her. This wasn't good. What in the hell was she doing here? With him? Was she out of her mind?

He strode across the great room, leaving Kelly to take in the sights and smells of his wonderful log cabin. A bank of tall windows at one end of the great room allowed sunlight to stream into the spacious open area and across dark hardwood floors. The ceiling was vaulted with fans slowly turning overhead in the exposed wooden rafters.

Kelly pivoted taking in the rustic charm of Rob's home with its two, brown leather sofas and an overstuffed, burnt orange chair. Magazines and books were scattered on the coffee table and on the floor beside the chair. Above the stone fireplace was the only bit of modern technology in the room, a large flat screen TV. The log cabin didn't fit the picture she'd created of him as a sophisticated Chicago lawyer.

At the opposite end of the room, a metal, spiral staircase led up to a loft that could be seen from the floor below. Behind the staircase was a galley kitchen, perfect for a single man. Rob was already there unloading groceries.

"Like my bachelor pad?" he asked not turning around when she came into the kitchen.

Kelly gazed out French doors to a patio and well-manicured yard beyond. "I must admit I didn't figure you for a log cabin kind of guy."

He turned to face her with a knowing look as if her response pleased him. "Surprised you, huh?"

"I should say so." She shrugged. "You didn't have this house when you were married, did you?"

"No." He turned back to the countertop, removed a carton of eggs, and folded the cloth bag. "We owned a house in Locust Grove close to my dad. I couldn't stay there."

Kelly glanced at him, hearing, once more, the hurt in his voice. What woman would divorce a guy like Rob? His ex-wife must be out of her mind.

Rob pulled a hand mixer and a glass bowl from a lower cabinet. "You'll have to do the honors," he said, "if you want this wedding cake to turn out right."

"You're assuming I can cook." She walked over beside him, trying to ignore the tingle of excitement racing through her body just because of his nearness.

"I figure you have many talents. I've already seen your pitching arm and how you sit a horse."

The memory of yesterday afternoon rushed back like gangbusters. Kelly felt her face grow warm. As she told Rachel, she had enjoyed that kiss a little too much. The ride back to the barn had been an erotic nightmare as her body felt on fire where it touched and rubbed the saddle. That she'd been without a good dose of sex for a long time had been all too apparent to her.

"Well, get out of the way, mister, if you want me to work on this cake." Kelly bumped Rob, aiming to tease him a little.

He didn't move, standing his ground so that their bodies touched. "Do you want my help?"

She swallowed hard. "No, get out of my kitchen!"

"My kitchen, remember." He pulled out one of the chairs from the small dining set by the French doors, turned it around and straddled it, resting his arms on the back. "I'll watch."

Kelly's body warmed and then throbbed as she struggled to ignore Rob's gaze upon her every action. She wore sandals and a blue, cotton and spandex sundress with a halter neckline, open at the back. Her legs and body were much too exposed to Rob's rapt attention.

Kelly couldn't remember the last time she'd made a cake, but it was like pitching or riding a horse, something not easily forgotten. Turning on the oven to heat, she greased the cake pans and dusted them with flour. With every move she made, she felt like a clumsy child, but she put her mind to it and slowly, methodically prepared the cake batter and poured it into the round baking pans.

When she picked up a cake pan to place it in the stainless steel oven, Rob jumped up and opened the door for her. He stood there while she retrieved the second pan and put it on the rack. Then he shut the oven door.

"How long?" he asked.

Kelly glanced at the box once more. "Thirty-five minutes."

Rob twisted the timer. "Done. Let's go sit down."

Kelly followed him into the great room and plopped down on the sofa, thinking he'd take the easy chair. Instead, he sat next to her and turned slightly toward her with his arm resting on the top of the sofa.

She shot him a questioning look. "What?"

"You're beautiful. You've always been beautiful."

The sincerity in his voice made her feel warm and cared for. She met his concerned gaze. "I bet you say that to all the girls," she said, trying to make light of his words.

"Not recently."

She attempted to change the subject and leaned forward picking up a book from the coffee table. "So what are you reading? *American Assassin.*"

"A Mitch Rapp thriller by Vince Flynn."

Kelly set the heavy hardback book down and glanced at him. "Do you read much?"

"Not much else to do in Heritage Springs for a single man."

"An *eligible* one," she reminded him.

"Not many single women to select from until you came to town."

Kelly avoided his heavy-lidded gaze and the hint of suggestion in his voice. No one in her family had made her feel loved for herself until Aunt Bess had taken her in. To Thomas, she had been a commodity, another teacher whom he let into his bed to satisfy his basic urges. After so many years, he probably had felt obligated to pop the question. She hadn't loved him. Once she had loved Rob.

Don't do this to yourself.

But her body refused to listen to reason. She settled back feeling the brush of his arm on her exposed back "I won't be in Heritage Springs much longer," she told him in a soft voice.

The muscle in his arm flexed. "Why not?"

"I have plans," she lied. "To start with, I'm going to visit friends in North Carolina on Saturday."

"You don't want to stick around? See your mother settled?"

"My mother needs no help from me. Your father is taking quite good care of her, better than I could ever do."

"How about sticking around to get to know me again?"

Air squeezed out of her lungs. "No way!" The words escaped from her in a breathless rush before she could stop them.

"I'm so terrible then?" He touched her bare neck. "Once you didn't think like that."

The tingle from where he touched her coursed throughout her body. "That was more than twenty years ago, Rob."

She scooted away, but he stopped her with his fingers on her shoulders, pressing her back toward his hard body. "What happened then, Kel? Why did you run away?"

Kelly tensed, her heart thudding wildly in her chest. "What do you mean, what happened? I got pregnant. Remember? My father wanted me to get an abortion. I wasn't going to do that."

Rob caught her chin and forced her to face him. His eyes were filled with curiosity and pain, a mixture of what he must be feeling. "I admit I didn't think about it at the time, but later, especially after Jess couldn't have children, I wondered if I was the father of your baby."

Her eyes rounded in alarm and a shudder of fear passed through her. She shook free of his touch. "Of course not." Her tone was sharp. "You weren't the only guy, you know?"

"I thought I was."

Kelly ignored the hurt she heard. "Well, don't kid yourself."

Rob sat quietly a moment as if absorbing what she had said. Kelly hated herself. Hated the big secret she kept. But there was no impulse to reveal the truth. She'd kept it so long from her father for fear of what he might do. She'd kept it from C.B. and even Aunt Bess. There was no possible way she could tell her mother the truth, especially now that she was marrying Rob's father. It was her secret to hold, now and forever.

Finally, Rob touched her again, pulling her into his arms as they sat there on his brown leather sofa. She was stiff, resisting, filled with fear and determination not to be overcome.

"Okay, the past is over. Let's forget it. Let's talk about the future."

"Future?"

"You and me."

A lump lodged in her throat. "We have no future."

"We could," he said in an offhanded way.

"I'm leaving town," she protested.

"Not until Saturday."

There was a promise and a threat in his response. Kelly searched his face. He wasn't kidding by the look in his eyes. Rob lowered his head to kiss her.

The timer buzzed in the kitchen.

"Saved by the bell!" Kelly ducked out of his arms and hurried away from him.

Grabbing a potholder, she opened the oven door and lifted the sweet-smelling strawberry cake from the racks. She placed each hot pan on cooling racks, closed the door and turned off the oven.

Rob was next to her by then, blocking her exit from the kitchen. He removed the potholder from her hand and tossed it toward the countertop. He missed, and it slid to the floor. Kelly caught the miss from the corner of her eye, but her attention was riveted on

Rob. He towered above her, the muscles in his arms visible because he was wearing a short-sleeved blue Polo shirt that matched the color of his eyes.

"I love you, Kelly."

"Rob!" she protested and tried to slide past him.

He grasped her arms, tugged her toward him. "I've loved you, Kelly, since the first moment I laid eyes on you. I married Jessica thinking she was just like you. But she wasn't. When Dad told me he was marrying your mother, I couldn't believe my luck. Here was my second chance with you. To have you back, to hold you, to love you once again is like a dream come true." There was a silent plea in his eyes. "Please, Kelly. Let me show you how much I love you."

"Rob," she said again, but this time with less force.

"Let me love you."

Now his voice was low and husky, heavy with desire that sparkled in his eyes. Electricity crackled between them. He caught her hips and pulled her against him. Her eyes widened when she felt his erection.

"You see what you do to me?"

Thomas had never spoken to her like that or pursued her with such intensity. The old Rob had never been like this either, always respecting her wishes about their hidden relationship. Their one night together had been the first for both of them.

Not any more. No, not any more.

Kelly reacted to his arousal like a mare ready for a stallion. She grew wet fast. Her whole body burned, especially in her most private place.

What am I going to do?

"Let me love you," he urged again.

Her breath turned shallow. She couldn't speak. She needed to get away while a shred of sanity remained.

His head dipped, and his mouth sought hers, greedily working over her lips, kissing her as if tomorrow would never come. She heard herself whimper.

Rob's hands investigated her hips, scrunching up the skirt of her dress and then dropping down to her cotton panties. He grabbed her bottom. Her body arched against him, seeking his hardness against her soft spot. She kissed him back with a bewildering passion that seemed to spring up from nowhere. It was as if she could not get enough of him, his taste, his feel, his heart.

"I have condoms in my bedroom," he murmured pulling her even closer, gripping her hard.

She wanted to jump inside his skin—be a part of him as she had so long ago. The ache, the drive was irresistible and she didn't resist. Saturday she would be gone. Today she needed this release, this closure. She could go to North Carolina with a clear mind, no longer wondering what if.

Kelly rocked against his erection. She took his face between her hands and drove her tongue into his mouth as frenzied in her desire as he.

"God, Kelly, I can stop now but not much longer if you keep this up."

"I don't want you to stop," she said gasping.

And he didn't.

CHAPTER TWELVE

Making love didn't change a thing, and it changed everything. Kelly still planned to leave on Saturday, and now she had even more reason to go.

Turning her head, Kelly peeped at Rob sleeping soundly beside her. They were lying in his king-sized bed, having spent the night together making love three times. She had counted them, wondering about the stamina of the man she had once loved and lost.

A sense of disbelief tore through her. Was she crazy? She licked her lips and turned on her side to stare at Rob's gray bedroom walls.

What must she have been thinking to have sex with Rob? Oh, that's right. She hadn't been thinking. Her urges had taken over, sweeping her away when he swept her into his arms and carried her to his bed.

Have I made the biggest mistake of my life?

Carefully, so not to wake him, Kelly eased the sheet back and crawled out of bed. Her panties were discarded on the hardwood floor. So were her sandals. Her bra was nowhere to be found. Kelly slipped on her panties and picked up the sandals. Padding out of the bedroom, she went through the great room and found her bra in the middle of the kitchen floor right next to her rumpled sundress.

Last night Rob had pulled the tie at the back of her neck and the bodice of her dress had slid down around her waist. He had unbuckled her belt and then the dress had fallen to the floor leaving her standing in front of him with her head held high. He had unsnapped her bra, lifting it off and kissed her non-stop, his hands moving, cupping, caressing, and stimulating her beyond caring. Even now her nerve endings felt on fire simply remembering.

Kelly put her bra back on and struggled into her dress. Turned toward the French doors and the bright morning sun streaming through them warming her face, she reached behind her neck to tie the halter.

"Let me help."

His deep voice sent chills skittering down her spine. His strong hands hovered near her neck tying the tie. She longed to lean back against his chest and experience his arms around her one more time, but she couldn't. Not now. Not ever again.

Without saying a word, Rob took matters into his own hands and hugged her against him, kissing the top of her head and squeezing her tight. "You feel so good," he murmured. "God, how I love you."

No, this wasn't right. She had made enough mess of things simply by sleeping with him.

When she didn't reply, he asked, "What are you doing up so early?"

"We never finished icing the cake." Kelly inclined her head toward the now cool pans. "And I need to get home. Today is my mother's wedding day."

"Ah, yes. I conveniently forgot." He let her go. "Can I help?"

"No." She turned to face him. He was naked.

Rob grinned down at her expression. "What? You've never seen a naked man before?"

"Not one as handsome as you," she said truthfully.

He cupped her face in his hands and kissed her hard, breaking off seconds later. "If I keep this up, I won't stop." He backed away. "I'll go get cleaned up and then take you home."

"Great." She was breathless. Bemused. Determined.

She offered him a half-hearted smile and turned back to the kitchen counter as if ready to ice the cake.

When she heard him leave, Kelly rocked against the counter and put her hands on the surface to steady herself. Deep in her heart she felt that familiar remorse and an ever-deeper sense of panic. She had lived with those feelings over twenty years, never getting closure or peace, always on the wrong side of things simply because of one big secret that hung around her neck like that dead albatross in the poem she'd read in college.

ROB TOOK her home but they didn't say much to each other on the way. Unaware of her lies and misgivings and the terrible dread she lived with, Rob wore a self-satisfied look, like a cat that had caught a mouse. He must think everything was fine, that they were starting to explore a new relationship. He loved her, he said. That was all that mattered.

"I'll take the cake on to Dad's and go to work for a while before I go back home and dress for the ceremony," Rob told her as he pulled up to the curb of her mother's house.

Kelly stilled for one heartbeat before turning to face Rob. His compelling blue eyes bore into hers as if stripping her naked or searching her soul. The shadow of his beard added to his ruggedly handsome, manly beauty while his tousled blond hair reminded her of a small boy. She couldn't help but smile at the thought.

Rob smiled back, reaching out to touch her chin, urging her lips toward his. She didn't want to kiss him but couldn't resist. Leaning forward, Kelly brushed his lips with hers, quivering at the gentleness of his kiss so full of poignancy and longing.

"We're good together, Kelly," he said when she sat back.

She glanced away, her heart hammering with recurring fear. "I've got to go."

"Yes," he murmured. "I'll see you this afternoon."

"Sure."

Kelly opened the door and climbed out of his Beemer. Almost sprinting to the house, she didn't want to think about his sudden declaration. She also didn't want to do this wedding thing. She wanted to run and hide. Turning the key, she let herself into her mother's cluttered living room.

Arms folded across her chest like a disapproving schoolmarm, Grace stood in the hallway blocking the way. "You didn't come home last night," she said.

Kelly hesitated, blinking with confusion. "I'm forty years old, Mother, for heaven sakes."

"You're in my house as a guest. I was worried about you."

"I was okay," Kelly said, brushing past her mother and stomping up the stairs to hide in her bedroom as if she was seventeen all over again.

Why did she turn into an idiotic teenager when she came into this house? Why did she act like she had never lived on her own and successfully raised a child? Kelly felt suddenly ill equipped to deal with her emotions. She sat down on her bed, shoulders slumping, and fought real terror that bubbled up from within.

Her mother came up the steps and stood in the doorway. This time her arms weren't folded. She looked sad and unhappy. Guilt raced through Kelly's heart. She shouldn't react like this with her mother. If it had been C.B. out all night, she would have been just as upset.

"I am getting married today," Grace said quietly. "It is the happiest day of my life, but I don't like seeing you so unhappy, Kelly."

"I'm not unhappy," Kelly replied, suddenly on the defensive.

But her mother would have none of it. "You most certainly are. I didn't have the strength to do anything about it when your father was alive, but I do now."

She joined Kelly on the bed and put a gentle hand on her daughter's bare knee. Kelly tried not to shrink at the touch. Where was this going? She fought down the compulsion to spring to her feet and flee the room.

"I want to apologize to you," her mother said in a voice so hushed that Kelly could hardly hear her words.

"Whatever for?" Still on the defensive, she didn't want to hear an apology.

"I didn't stick up for you when you got pregnant."

Kelly made a dismissing gesture with her hand. "That was a long time ago, Mother."

"But it's still eating away at you, dear. I know it. You don't have to say anything for a mother to know."

"Well, it's my problem." Kelly tried to sidestep the issue. "I'll deal with it."

Grace's fingers pressed Kelly's knee. "It's my problem as well. I want to start my new life with the demons from my past exorcized."

"Oh, come on, Mother," Kelly scoffed. "You don't have any demons."

"I have secrets just as you do, Kelly."

Kelly's lips parted in surprise. "You're the most self-effacing woman I know. What possible demons can you have to hide?"

"Your father was a hard man, but a good man." Grace cast her gaze downward. "But I didn't love him."

"That's your secret?" Kelly wasn't shocked by her mother's admission. She had found her father hard to love as well.

Grace withdrew her hand to rub her temple. "Your father loved you, Kelly. That's why he was strict when you were growing up. He thought if he could control your clothing, your friends, and activities, he could protect you."

Kelly crossed her arms as if to shield herself from old anger and resentment. Her mother was right. It still churned in her belly as roughly as it had over twenty years ago.

"And then you got pregnant," Grace's voice died away.

"Best mistake I ever made," Kelly said sharply, tired of defending what *had* turned out to be the most wonderful thing in her life—her daughter.

"But you see," Grace said. "That's exactly what he was trying to prevent."

"I'm sorry I disappointed him." The sarcasm rang in her voice because Kelly wasn't sorry. She was defiant in her anger.

Grace's eyes brimmed with tears. Her lower lip quivered. "But he was disappointed, you see, because it's just exactly what had happened to us."

Kelly's heart stilled. She turned to stare at her mother.

"I had to marry your father, Kelly." Grace paused, letting her words sink in "Because I was pregnant with you."

CHAPTER THIRTEEN

Friday afternocn
Five o'clock

In a corner of Howie's living room, a four-piece string quartet played soft chamber music. The furniture had been removed and replaced with folding chairs arranged in a semi-circle facing the floor-to-ceiling windows. The plantation shutters had been shut to provide a backdrop of white, and in front of them, a table held a cascading arrangement of yellow and lavender roses and other flowers Rob couldn't name.

His aunt and her husband, his four cousins and their spouses, were already seated. The minister and his dad were in the kitchen where Howie was making life difficult for the caterer and her staff. The ceremony cnly waited for the arrival of Kelly's daughter and husband who were stuck in traffic on I-64 coming out of Louisville.

"They're five minutes out," Kelly said coming down the steps to the foyer.

Rob looked up and for the first time since he dropped Kelly off this morning and knew he gazed upon the love of his life. The thought resonated for him, seeming right, as if meant to be. Sure, he was taking a giant leap of faith with this relationship. Kelly was hesitant, not committing to him. He knew that. But he had committed last night, if only in his mind, heart, and soul. She was what he wanted. Needed.

He must convince Kelly of that need.

"I'd give you a wolf whistle if it wasn't for the guests," he said nodding his head toward the living room where his family waited.

"What?" Kelly reached the bottom of the stairs and peered at him as if not understanding.

"A wolf whistle to let you know you're beautiful."

And she was—wearing a royal blue, V-neck, sleeveless dress that hit just above the knee and fitted her figure like a glove. Her legs were bare and she wore black, high-heel pumps. Diamond teardrop earrings dangled from her ears.

She blushed. "Don't."

"Don't what? Compliment you? You're the most beautiful forty-year-old woman I've ever laid my eyes on."

"Now, really don't!" A glint of humor returning, her eyes flashed. "I don't like to be reminded."

He chuckled. "I can't help myself."

She grimaced and swatted his arm playfully. "Women don't want to talk about their ages."

"I'll remember," Rob conceded.

"Oh, good grief. Who dressed you?"

"What do you mean?"

"Who put on that boutonnière? It's crooked and too low."

"Howie." Rob shrugged. "Will you fix it?"

"Of course, I can't let you wear it like that."

Kelly stepped nearer and unpinned the white rose on his lapel. She smelled of vanilla, subtle but sweet. His body throbbed with desire at her touch. Could he convince her to come home with him again tonight? Could he make her understand that leaving her years ago was the biggest mistake of his life?

KELLY PINNED Rob's boutonnière to the lapel of his navy Brooks Brothers' suit, an intimate action that she found disconcerting, to say the least. Her fingers tingled on the finely woven Italian wool as she drank in the subtle masculine scent of Rob's aftershave. He wore a light blue, traditional shirt with French cuffs and a silk navy and light blue paisley tie. He looked mighty handsome.

But not as handsome as you look in the flesh.

She wasn't bold enough to tell him that. In fact, there was nothing bold about her at the moment. Only hours earlier, she had come to a sort of closure with her mother. In a small way, she was able to forgive her father and feel sorry for her mother, who had put up with a bad marriage, in part for Kelly's sake.

That she could be truly happy for her mother and her upcoming nuptials was a good thing. That they could hug and make up was the best. Yet it had been hard to soften her heart for fear that if she did, somehow her mother would stab it again. But she risked it. For once.

The bad part was to come—when Rob faced his daughter for the first time. The daughter he didn't know existed.

The doorbell rang almost on cue. Kelly turned. Heart in her throat, she stood fixed in her spot watching Rob go to the door.

"You must be C.B.," Rob said swinging it open wide. "And you're Daniel." He offered his hand to the younger man. "I'm Rob Scott, Howie's son,"

"I would know you anywhere," C.B. said in her cheerful, perky way. "Gran described you to me."

"She did?"

"Yes, she did. She seems to think you would be just the right man for my mother."

"C.B.!" Kelly exclaimed, horrified.

"Mom!" Smiling, C.B. rushed into the room and hugged her. "You look so pretty."

"You do too, pumpkin."

Rob shut the door behind Daniel, who came in and gave Kelly a hug. When Daniel stepped back to take C.B.'s hand in a possessive display of ownership, Kelly got the message. So that was the way it would be between them? Both of them vying for C.B.'s affection?

"I have to agree with your grandmother," Rob was saying. "She has excellent powers of observation."

C.B. laughed and then stuck out her hand. "I'm glad to meet you, anyway, Mr. Scott, and I'm glad my grandmother is going to be in your family."

Rob took her hand. Their handshake connected them in what they must believe to be a fun-loving conspiracy. But it was more than that. Much more.

Am I the only one to notice the resemblance?

Kelly drew in a breath and held it, fearing Daniel would burst out with the truth because he was watching his wife and Rob closely.

She cleared her throat and said, "I think you two had better take your seats. They want to get started."

"Oh, yes," C.B. agreed.

She and Daniel walked hand in hand into the living room leaving Kelly alone with Rob. Heart beating fast, she gazed up at him. Did he suspect anything? He would almost have to be blind not to notice.

"You're daughter is beautiful, Kelly."

"Yes, she is."

"You're very lucky."

His words pierced her to the core. She swallowed hard. "I don't know about that," she said, dismissing him. "I do know if I don't get back upstairs to the bride, I'll never be forgiven."

With that she turned and fled up the stairs, once more evading the truth and what might turn out to be inevitable.

THE SMALL, intimate wedding concluded without a hitch. Rob stood up for his father, and Kelly—carrying a small, hand tied bouquet of white roses—acted as her mother's maid of honor. Afterwards, everyone followed the newlyweds outside to the garden where the caterer had set up a dinner complete with a choice of filet mignon or salmon. The string quartet transferred their chairs and instruments to the garden and continued playing the soft, soothing music.

"I see my new stepmother is serious about matchmaking," Rob whispered to Kelly, who was seated by his side. His engraved place card was situated next to hers.

Kelly paused taking a bite of her Caesar salad. "Maybe she'll have other things to think about now that she is married." Her tone was dry and not amused.

"I like the way her mind works," Rob said.

Kelly swallowed her bite. "She should *mind* her own business."

"Ah, you sound upset." He enjoyed teasing her. "Join me at my house tonight, and we can discuss the cause."

Shooting him a hard look, Kelly dug into her salad.

"You can't deny you enjoyed last night as much as I did," he said.

"I'm ignoring you." She took a drink of iced tea and deliberately turned her head to speak to her mother.

Kelly couldn't ignore him forever. Rob let up, hiding a self-satisfied smile, and sat back in his chair. The guests were seated at a large round table covered by a white tablecloth. C.B. and her husband sat on the opposite side of the table so that Rob had a clear view of Kelly's daughter.

He had expected C.B. to have Kelly's red hair, but it was blond. She had two cute dimples when she smiled and a pert little nose that was more pixie-like than Kelly's. As he sipped a vodka and water, he watched her interaction with Daniel and one of his cousins on her right. There was something familiar about her. Something that made him remember his grandmother.

Rob sat up and placed his glass on the table. The question that was forming in his mind seemed so out of this world impossible. He fought for breath and for the quieting of his racing heart.

Could C.B. be his daughter?

Kelly had denied it. He'd flat out asked her, and she'd said no. Now he wondered

Rob picked up his glass again and brought it to his lips. Slowly, he took a sip and stared at C.B. over the rim as he struggled to tamp down his growing excitement.

It was safe to say C.B. didn't know who he was. And no, he couldn't ask Kelly again, not after she'd told him no. What if he got his hopes up only to learn C.B. was not his daughter?

Rob didn't think he could survive the disappointment.

CHAPTER FOURTEEN

Would the evening ever end? The newlyweds seemed in no hurry to leave the reception, and the strain of having C.B. and Rob together frayed Kelly's nerves. She had watched them dance, suffering every step as they twirled around the garden dance area. And then Rob had danced with her. When he took her into his arms, she thought she would melt into the garden path.

Kelly wanted him, but she couldn't allow herself to give in. Happily-ever-after endings never happened to her. It was enough to know her mother and C.B. were happy. That was as much as she could wish for, given the secret she carried and the mistakes she'd made.

It was approaching nine o'clock when she missed seeing Rob in the garden. C.B. was gone too. Daniel chatted with her mother at the dining table where the twilight was now lit by glowing candlelight. That Rob and C.B. were not in sight troubled her, so Kelly slipped into the house

She found C.B. in the upstairs guest bathroom repairing her makeup. Joining her daughter at the double sinks, Kelly smoothed down her hair and washed her hands.

"It's been a nice wedding," she said. This was the first time she'd been alone with C.B. in a long time.

"Oh, yes! And Gran is so happy. Howie is such a nice man."

"Yes." Kelly nodded. "I expect he's going to treat her better than my father ever did."

C.B. looked thoughtful. "Gran deserves it. She's put up with a lot." Turning to the mirror, she said, "You too, Mom. You deserve a nice guy like that."

"I don't know. Maybe some day."

"What about Rob?" C.B. asked. "He seems to like you."

"I guess."

"Why don't you do something about it? I bet if you chase him a little, you can catch him."

Kelly smiled, hoping her smile covered her uneasiness. "You sound just like your grandmother. Matchmaking must run in the family."

C.B. returned a pout. "I don't know why you make a joke about it. You don't need to worry about me now. Besides, you're not young any more. You're forty years old."

"Don't remind me."

"It's time you do something for yourself, Mom. Stop playing the martyr."

A tense silence surrounded them. Kelly's chest felt as if it would burst. "Is that what you think I am?"

C.B. glanced at Kelly's image in the mirror. "I think you have sacrificed enough," she said softly. "I think it's time for you to let go of me and get on with your life."

Kelly suddenly burned with anger. "That's Daniel talking."

"What if it is?" C.B. lifted her chin. "He's my husband, and he's right most of the time."

"But he doesn't know anything about me. What right does he have to pass judgment?"

C.B. turned to her. "It's not judgment. He cares about me, and he cares about you. He knows it's time for us to change our relationship. I'm all grown up, Mom. I'm married."

Kelly wanted to run and hide. Her insides felt like jelly, mixed with anger and fear and an extra dose of confusion. "Why attack me all of a sudden? We always had such a good relationship, C.B. You, Aunt Bess, and me. What have I done to change that?"

C.B.'s lip quivered, but she stood her ground. "You see the Scott family out there? Happy? Together? Daniel's family is like that. It's a big family. I've always wanted a big family. Like everybody else."

Kelly licked her lips. Her hands were cold. She clutched them, her fingernails biting into her palms. "Not everyone has big families, C.B. I did the best I could."

"Did you? Then why won't you tell me who my father is? What's so terrible about him? Can't you get it through your head I've always thought he didn't want me?"

"That's not true, C.B. Your father doesn't know about you." Kelly's voice was shaky. "I never told him."

C.B. straightened her shoulders. "I don't understand you."

"I had my reasons." Kelly dropped her gaze.

"Fine." There was a new hardness in C.B.'s tone. "One more thing, if you please." She took a breath. "My name is not C.B. I'm no longer Colleen Baron but Mrs. Daniel Lyons. You can stop calling me C.B."

Her daughter swept past in a hurry. "C.B.!" Kelly reached for her, but her precious child left the bathroom and didn't look back.

"Colleen," Kelly whispered and slumped against the sink, feeling anguish so deep that it threatened to overcome her remaining control.

~

KELLY WALKED zombie-like down the staircase to the entrance foyer. Outside the candlelit garden was a-buzz with music and activity. Inside however, the rooms were shadowy and quiet in the growing dusk.

She paused and drew a deep breath trying to mollify the jumbled emotions coursing through her heart and mind. With no place left to hide, Kelly faced a dilemma. Did she tell the truth? Was it too late? Would C.B.—Colleen—and Rob ever forgive her?

Her instinct said no. She must continue to keep her secret. It was her default position. She knew nothing else. Kelly rubbed her damp palms down the slick skirt of her royal blue dress.

What am I going to do?

A movement in the living room drew her attention. She glanced into the dark room and recognized Rob sitting silently in the shadows facing the huge flower arrangement where the wedding had taken place. He was slumped forward with his elbows on his knees and his hands clasped. When she sat down beside him, he didn't move.

An inscrutable silence followed. Kelly inhaled sharply as it lengthened. Had he learned the truth? What was wrong? Sensing his tension, she touched his shoulder.

Rob aroused long enough to glance her way. His face was ashen, his blue eyes glassy.

"God, Kelly," he said in a voice that could break a heart.

For a split second, Kelly wanted to run, but this was Rob. Something troubled him.

"What's wrong?" She dreaded the answer, but she couldn't leave him.

He sat back in the chair and stared at the ceiling. Finally, he said, "Jessica is pregnant."

"What?" Kelly placed her hand on his knee. "You told me she didn't want children."

Rob rubbed a hand down his face. "After she miscarried, she told me she didn't want to be a mother. She made me feel guilty as if it was my fault she lost the baby. She called me a failure. It's the one thing I wanted that I could never have."

"But she's pregnant now?"

"Yes, second trimester. It didn't take her new husband long to do what I couldn't do in ten years. And of course, she called tonight to gloat. The bitch."

Rob's anger was laced with sorrow and regret. Kelly understood. A woman he loved had betrayed him.

Just as I betrayed him so many years ago.

No! She'd been the victim! Wronged by Rob's mother and then her father—a casualty of circumstances. She had been the one who had lived with the mistake.

And the one who had reaped the reward, for Colleen Baron had been the prize of a lifetime, a gift Rob had never been given.

Kelly removed her hand from Rob's knee and stirred uneasily in the chair. "Life's not fair," she said in a voice she hardly recognized.

"You can say that again." He brushed a gaze full of bitterness across her face.

"I'm sorry," she whispered.

He sat up straight, manning up. "It doesn't matter. I'll get over it."

"But you shouldn't have to. Jessica shouldn't treat you like this. You don't deserve it, Rob." Her annoyance increased. "You would have been a wonderful father."

"Like you are a wonderful mother." For an instant his glance sharpened.

Kelly dropped her gaze afraid to meet his eyes. "I don't know about that."

"I know. C.B. is proof of the good job you did."

"Colleen," Kelly muttered. "She wants to be called 'Colleen.'"

"You don't give yourself enough credit." He reached out and caught her hand in his. "You've found the strength inside to go it alone under difficult circumstances. You not only survived but thrived. You're a remarkable woman, Kelly Baron."

Dangerously close to tears, Kelly shook her head and pulled her hand away.

"Come home with me tonight, Kel. I love you. I need you."

She looked up, disoriented. There was vulnerability in his eyes she had never seen before. No, she had to cut him off. Life *wasn't* fair.

She had already done enough damage where Rob was concerned. She wasn't worthy of his misplaced trust and love.

"I can't." Her voice rose sounding steely. "I'm leaving for North Carolina bright and early in the morning."

THE PARTY BROKE up thirty minutes later. Mr. and Mrs. Howard Scott left for their honeymoon to a chorus of well wishes and a shower of rose petals. Colleen and Daniel left to return home. There was strain in their departure, a strain that broke Kelly's heart.

After the other relatives said their goodbyes, Rob and Kelly were alone except for the catering staff doing the clean up.

"Go home, Kelly," Rob ordered in a tired voice devoid of emotion. "I'll straighten up and lock the doors after the caterer is done."

Kelly glanced around the bright living room. The earlier shadows were gone. "Okay, if you think I'm not needed."

"No," he said with a pointed stare. "You're not needed. Not many chances I'll screw this up."

She dropped her eyes before his steady gaze and battled with overwhelming remorse. "I'll see you then."

"Sure." Rob turned his back.

Nothing remained for her to do but walk to her car and drive away.

HER MOTHER'S house was dark and uninviting. The ghost-like boxes in the living room stacked for Rob's yard sale filled the room with a disembodied presence and contributed to the eerie silence. Kelly mounted the stairs to her bedroom. She changed out of her fancy dress into shorts and a T-shirt.

Should she start for North Carolina tonight? Kelly truly didn't know what to do. Her life had no purpose. Or hope.

Without hope, what do I have?

Her shoulders sagged under the weight of her anguish. Legs collapsing under her, Kelly sank to her bed, wrapped her arms around herself and cried. Sobs wracked her body. She lowered her head to her pillow, pulled her legs up, curling in a fetal position, and poured out her sorrow until there were no tears left.

Rob was hurting. It was her fault. Her nurturing instinct compelled her to make it better, as if she could kiss his bruises and make the pain go away.

How? She had no power. No control, and she didn't trust the outcome.

A far-away voice rang in her ears. "Believe in yourself, Kelly," her great-aunt had said, urging her to take risks.

But believing had always been hard. Kelly had always felt vulnerable. Inadequate.

"You don't give yourself enough credit," Rob had told her. "You're a remarkable woman."

Rob had recognized her lack of self-confidence. Aunt Bess too. Her mother knew she was unhappy and tried to help. Even Rachel had pinpointed her fear of taking action. "Life just doesn't happen," Rachel had said. "You must create what you want out of it."

What do I want?

Kelly sat up and wiped away her tears. She was sick from the struggle within and longed for peace and closure…and love.

I want Rob.

"I bet if you chase him a little, you can catch him," Colleen had suggested.

Staring at the empty walls, Kelly knew the only way she could ever catch Rob was to tell him the truth. It was a risk. He might hate her. Yet anything was better than the empty, soulless life she was leading.

She sucked in a huge breath. Telling Rob meant telling Colleen. Could she face her daughter's anger? Kelly shut her eyes.

She had faced Colleen's anger tonight. As Rob said, she had survived.

I've always survived.

Kelly opened her eyes and climbed to her feet. She needed to ease Rob's hurt and help him understand he wasn't a failure. He had a child, a beautiful daughter who needed him as much as he needed her.

Maybe somewhere in this mess, Kelly could create a new future from the ashes of the past.

CHAPTER FIFTEEN

The night was hot and sticky. No air moved in the darkness. Only a few fireflies flickered among the trees as Kelly turned off her headlights and climbed out of her car.

Fear cramped her stomach, and her limbs felt weak. Her sandals crunching on the gravel path, she could hardly walk toward Rob's log cabin. The distant noise of insects buzzing in the dead, country silence was the only other sound she heard.

Kelly stepped up one short step to the front porch and pushed the doorbell without hesitation. If she thought about it, she might turn away. Sucking in a huge breath, Kelly waited, rocking back on her heels and trying to control her trepidation.

The door opened. Light from the great room flooded the porch, blinding Kelly for a moment. Rob stood quietly at the threshold, surprise glinting in his eyes until he hid it behind hooded eyelashes.

"You invited me," Kelly said, her voice cracking.

Rob stared until her skin prickled. When he didn't speak, she asked, "May I come in?"

He stepped back from the door. Kelly marched past him with a confidence she didn't feel. She turned in the middle of the great room and watched Rob slowly shut the front door.

He turned and made eye contact. She fought to keep her chin high and shoulders squared.

How do I tell him? What do I say?

"I thought you were leaving." His statement was an indictment.

Kelly cleared her throat. "I am. But I have something to tell you first."

He nodded toward the sofa. "Have a seat."

Kelly sat down hard, feeling as uncomfortable as a grade school kid in the principal's office. She clutched her hands in her lap. This time Rob took the easy chair, pushing back and propping his feet on the ottoman, as if he had no care in the world.

This didn't bode well. "I don't know where to begin," she said, begging for his understanding.

"Start at the beginning."

He gave no quarter, not in his posture or his direct gaze.

Heart surging into her throat, Kelly hesitated, looking away. She wrung her hands.

Get on with it. You came to confess. Do it!

Eyes remaining downcast in fear, she said softly, "I learned something on this trip home." Kelly glanced up at Rob's stony face. "My mother confessed something to me before she married your father."

He said nothing. She dropped her gaze again to her hands.

"She told me that she and my father had to get married because she was pregnant with me." Kelly raced on, "And that's why he treated me the way he did while I was growing up. He didn't want the same thing to happen to me."

Rob dropped his feet to the floor and sat up. She had his attention. "That's why he made you wear those ugly clothes and stupid hair style?"

Kelly nodded. "Yes."

"But you got pregnant anyway."

Kelly nodded again. Feeling her heart contract with the weight of her admission, she moved uneasily on the sofa. "Ironic, isn't it?"

"It is a cruel irony." Rob stood up and crossed over to the sofa. He sat down next to her and took her hand, squeezing it gently.

She straightened her back and looked away. "He was angry with me and disappointed. I can see that now."

"You didn't deserve his anger. I can't believe he wanted you to get an abortion. I would never have asked that of you."

Kelly's lower lip quivered. "Oh, God, Rob. I've so misjudged you."

He caressed her cheek. "No crying now. It's over."

"I haven't told you everything." Tears pooled in her eyes.

"I'm listening."

"I've never said this out loud to anyone. I don't know how to tell you."

Rob pulled her toward him, wrapping her in his arms. She snuggled close, feeling the rapid beat of his heart. His action gave her strength to go on.

"I did so many things wrong back then, Rob," Kelly admitted with a sob. "I deceived everyone, and once I started on that path, I didn't—couldn't—deviate. I thought only about C.B., ah, Colleen. I had to keep her safe. I had to protect her."

"You did a wonderful job," Rob murmured and kissed her forehead.

"But I should have done it differently. I couldn't. Not then. Not at eighteen. Not after your mother warned me away from you."

"My mother?"

Kelly tried to draw away, but he wouldn't let her go, continuing to hold her in his arms. She started to cry—long, heaving sobs that took her breath away. "Oh, God, Rob, I've hurt you and C.B. so much. It wasn't fair, but I didn't know what else to do."

Rob didn't speak, but there was a noticeable shift in his posture—a pause as if he knew what was coming.

"Before you went away to college, your mother had told me to stay away from you. My father wanted C.B. dead." Words tumbled from Kelly's lips. "The only person who understood was Aunt Bess. So I just packed my bags one day and got on a bus to Louisville. Aunt Bess took me in."

She made one more try to pull away. Rob's arms were like steel bands holding her. "Oh, Rob, it could have been different. I see that now. I shouldn't have lied to you. I know now you would have done the right thing."

She felt Rob's breathing hitch. He put his hands on her shoulders and gently pushed her back so he could look in her eyes.

"What are you saying to me, Kelly?" he asked quietly.

Kelly placed a hand to his T-shirt, feeling the wet spot she'd made with her tears. "I'm trying to tell you that Colleen is your child."

"But you said there were others." Rob's hushed voice held disbelief.

She shook her head. "There never was anyone else. Only you. I lied. I was afraid you'd hate me for never telling you."

He didn't say anything.

She pushed back, curling her trembling fingers into the fabric of the T-shirt as she raised her gaze to his face. "Maybe you do hate me. I'll understand if you do." Kelly swallowed hard. "I'm sorry, Rob" She drew in a deep shuddering breath. "Maybe I better go now."

"I'm a father?"

She nodded and wiped away her tears. "Yes."

"Colleen?"

"Yes."

"I thought she looked like my grandmother." His smile radiated down on Kelly. "I *knew* I was the only one in high school."

"Yes." She smiled up at him.

"My God, Kelly, I'm really a father?"

Nodding again, Kelly touched his cheek. "I'm sorry you've lost so many years. I'm sorry you never knew our daughter before tonight."

He caught her hand and kissed it. "I can't believe this! But I do believe it, because I believe in you, back in high school and today. Kelly Baron, you are one remarkable, loving woman."

Shame rushed through her. She didn't deserve his words. "I did the best I could."

"I should have been there for you." Rob squeezed her hand.

"You didn't know."

He shook his head. "I should have suspected, but when you never came to me, it was easier to assume I had nothing to do with your baby."

Rob dropped her hand and ran his fingers through his hair, tousling his blond locks like a small, anxious boy. "My mother was a strong woman. You know that. She had big plans for me, and it was easier to go with the flow. I'm sorry she hassled you, Kel. If I'd known, I might have mustered some courage, but I sorely lacked it at the time." He took a breath. "I might have stood up to my mother and things would be different today."

Rob kissed her, his fingers cupping her face, his lips demanding and quick, full of emotion and longing. "I'm so sorry, Kelly, for screwing up your life."

"You didn't screw up my life," she replied. "I had Colleen."

"You're too generous." Rob gazed lovingly into her eyes. "I'm at fault in this too." Kissing her once more, he murmured, "Marry me."

"Marry you?" she muttered back, hardly understanding or daring to hope.

"I have to marry the mother of my child."

"But she's all grown up."

"All the better." He kissed her long and hard. "We don't have to deal with diapers."

Kelly choked and pulled away. "Are you crazy?"

"No, serious."

"Seriously?" She shuddered as hope fluttered in her heart.

"I've never been more serious in my life."

Joy overcoming her, Kelly threw her arms around Rob's neck. He surrounded her with his embrace, and for the first time in her life, Kelly felt safe and secure. She liked that feeling. She was finally home.

"I suppose I'll have to call Rachel and tell her I'm not coming to North Carolina," Kelly said already thinking ahead.

"You'd better." His fingers found the front-clasp of her bra under her T-shirt.

The heat and vitality of the man pulsed against her sensitive breasts. She gasped a breath. "Then I suppose we'd better go to Louisville and talk to Colleen."

"We will," he said, pressing his lips against hers again in a needy affirmation. "Tomorrow."

Kelly gasped again. "Tomorrow."

"I love you, Kelly Baron."

"I love you too, Rob Scott."

EPILOGUE

One year later
Louisville

"We're an alert-looking bunch," Kelly drawled, smile on her lips and happiness in her heart. She looked down at Grace, Howie, and Daniel's parents who sat in a line of maternity waiting room chairs. Every tired eye was focused on the door to the labor and delivery rooms.

Rob sat at the end of the line, his long legs stretched out in front of him. She handed him a frosty can of Coke from the vending machine and sat down beside him in a hard hospital chair.

After nine long months, three with morning sickness, Colleen was finally in labor. The whole family had been waiting since noon, spending time in the labor room with the expectant couple until being asked to leave forty minutes earlier. First babies were notorious for taking their sweet time, but this one, apparently was on his or her way.

Part of tonight's excitement was the suspense of learning the gender of the new baby. Colleen and Daniel had insisted on being old-fashioned and had refused to find out during the routine ultrasound. They had wanted to be surprised, but it was killing Kelly.

"It's two o'clock," Howie complained, "and long past my bedtime. I'm usually in a prone position this time of the morning."

"Hush!" Grace slapped his sleeve in a good-humored way. "You're here to support your granddaughter."

"I can do that just as well at home," Howie growled, but Kelly was sure he didn't mean it from the twinkle in his eyes.

Angling her chair, Kelly clutched Rob's arm and put her head on his shoulder, nuzzling against his sleeve. He felt good and solid, so safe and secure. She loved him so much. Could her dream really have come true? Sometimes she just couldn't believe it.

And she couldn't believe her little girl—*their* daughter—was actually making them grandparents.

A year ago they had broken the news to Colleen, who had held Daniel's hand and wept. Kelly and Rob had wept too. It had been an emotional moment. And then Rob had been frantic to catch up. He wanted to know everything about his daughter, and Colleen wanted to share everything with him. Kelly had pulled out scrapbooks and photo albums from boxes in storage. There had been home movies to watch and stories to tell. Rob couldn't get enough of his child and learning about the childhood he had missed. Colleen had blossomed from Rob's attention, his acceptance…his love.

Finally, after a week in Louisville, Rob had taken Kelly back to his log cabin and made love to her as if he couldn't get enough of her either. He insisted she move in. Grace's sad, little house was left vacant for a while until Rachel came up from North Carolina for a visit and talked them into turning it into a bed and breakfast. After remodeling it, Rob hired Tara and Courtney's mother to run it, giving the single mother a job that left her plenty of time for her children.

In October, Rob had taken Kelly to Gatlinburg. Amid the falling leaves and roaring mountain streams, they were married, for better or worse, richer or poorer.

They had their ups and downs, oh yes. Who wouldn't? Two people, strangers really, trying to mesh their single lives into a workable union.

But it *was* working in a most beautiful way. And Kelly's life had changed dramatically. She now volunteered at the children's club in the afternoons. She took riding lessons, and Rob had bought her a Saddlebred mare of her very own. They traveled, too, flying to Greece and Italy. Rob told her he was finally doing all the things he was always too busy to do.

Yes, life was so much better today.

Kelly exhaled a long sigh of contentment and gave Rob's arm another squeeze. A year ago, she would never have believed creating a new life could be so easy. All she had to do was find Rob again.

Finding Rob caused her to truly find herself.

"Here he comes!"

Rob and Kelly jumped to their feet.

Daniel strode into the waiting room, a smile the length of a football field spreading across his face. He pulled a blue ball cap from behind his back and placed it firmly on his head. His mother took a step forward, her arms outstretched toward her son.

"It's a boy!" Daniel shouted. "I'm a father at last!"

As the rest of the family cheered and crowded around Daniel for details, Rob looked down at Kelly and smiled. "It took me a long time to become a father," he said. "Something tells me being a grandfather will be just as special."

"And this time," Kelly said with fierce determination, "we'll be grandparents together."

"At last." Rob hugged her tight. "Together, a family at last."

The End

I HOPE you enjoyed Kelly and Rob's story. Please consider sharing your experience with your fellow readers by leaving a review.

MORE ABOUT THE BLUEGRASS
HOMECOMING SERIES

To my readers...

I wrote the novel *Secrets* a few years ago, choosing to explore a romance about a woman caught between the past and her desire to explore her future. I wanted to submit the manuscript to a traditional publisher, but was advised, at the time, this publisher did not like forty-year-old heroines. Since then, "seasoned" romance has come into wider acceptance.

After changing the setting of the story, *Secrets* became the second book in my new Bluegrass Homecoming series, a series that will let me again explore the themes of second chances in the Bluegrass of Kentucky.

To start my new series, I've written about the love story of baby boomers Howie and Grace. Their granddaughter C.B. takes center stage in the third book, *Nom de Plume*.

I foresee more books in the series, because there are many characters in *Secrets* begging to have their own stories.

Happy reading,
Jan
www.janscarbrough.com

ABOUT THE AUTHOR

Jan Scarbrough writes heartwarming contemporary romances about second chances, single moms and children, and if the plot allows, about another passion—horses. Living in the horse country of Kentucky makes it easy for Jan to add small town, Southern charm to her books and the excitement of a Bluegrass horse race or a big-time, competitive horse show.

With author Maddie James, Jan has written the Montana McKenna series, the story of the family of James McKenna, a Montana rancher whose death changes the lives of his wife and children.

Leaving her contemporary voice behind, Jan wrote *My Lord Raven*, a medieval story of honor and betrayal, soon to be released, and *Freely Given*, a collection of short Medieval romances. Her paranormal Gothic romance, *Tangled Memories*, was a Romance Writers of America (RWA) Golden Heart finalist. *Timeless* is her latest paranormal romance.

A member of Novelist, Inc., Jan has published with Kensington, Five Star, ImaJinn Books, Resplendence Publishing, and Turquoise Morning Press. She has written over twenty-two books.

Here are some ways you can connect with Jan Scarbrough.

NOM DE PLUME: BLUEGRASS HOMECOMING

BOOK 3 - EXCERPT

When the dream of happily-ever-after is shattered, sometimes another door opens.

Friday Morning
Louisville, Kentucky

"Eat your oatmeal, Scotty," Colleen Lyons said with a mother's practiced voice.

The blond-haired boy stabbed at his gooey oatmeal with a spoon, preferring to pound the table with the end of his utensil rather than use it for eating. Tomorrow her son turned three. It hardly seemed possible. Time had flown so fast. Colleen cast a loving glance at Scotty before she turned to the kitchen counter where the one-cup coffee maker hissed as it finished brewing.

After pouring a generous amount of cream into the steaming cup of coffee, Colleen carried it to the table and placed it near her husband Daniel. He gazed at the morning paper without looking up, without acknowledging her helpfulness. That was all right. She didn't work outside the home, after all, and being a housewife and mother meant she did additional duties, relieving Daniel of responsibility. He attended med school and needed time to study.

Life would be better once his schooling was complete, but that would be several years away. She could wait. Just as she waited on him daily, Colleen had patience enough for both of them. Nevertheless, she often imagined the future. It was like a shiny object just beyond her reach—Daniel in the pediatric practice with his father, Scotty going off to middle school, and maybe another child to care for, a daughter this time. She'd always wanted a big family.

Yet, there were times when Colleen bit her tongue. Like now. Daniel looked a mess. His hair was tousled and his rheumy eyes rimmed with dark circles. He remained in his pajamas—a loose-fitting Louisville Cardinals T-shirt and gray sweat pants.

She turned back to the stove where bacon sizzled. "I wish you'd drive to Heritage Springs tomorrow for Scotty's birthday party."

Using a fork to remove the bacon, Colleen drained it on a paper towel. Then she scrambled free-range eggs in a frying pan that didn't have bacon grease in it. Daniel loved an old-fashioned breakfast. Cooking for him had been part of their routine since they met in college.

Putting the plate of food beside his paper, Colleen waited for a response. When none came, she drew her mouth into a rigid line. She never challenged Daniel, never complained. But when it came to Scotty, Colleen sometimes gathered her courage to speak.

"Did you hear me?"

Daniel looked up. "What?"

"I said I wished you'd take a break and come to Scotty's birthday party tomorrow."

"You know I can't," Daniel said. "I have a big exam in two weeks."

"I know." Colleen's shoulders slumped. "I was hoping you'd find the time. Scotty only turns three once. You're always studying and away from home."

"We've discussed this, Colleen. My education comes first. It's important to this family."

Colleen surveyed him with disappointment. He had already turned his attention back to the newspaper. Her husband was doing his best. Becoming a doctor like his father was important to Daniel— to all of them. She fought back a stab of guilt. She shouldn't complain. It wasn't good to nag. She needed to be supportive.

"Aren't you going to eat your breakfast?" Colleen asked with a sigh.

"What?" Daniel glanced up again. "Oh, yes. Sure."

He laid down the paper and slowly moved the breakfast plate in front of him. Colleen noticed his hands shake as he picked up a slice of bacon.

"I don't think you're getting enough sleep." The observation simply slipped out because it was natural for her to worry.

"I'm okay," he mumbled, stabbing at his eggs like Scotty played with his oatmeal. "I have to study, you know?"

"Yes, I know."

Still Colleen felt a niggling disquiet. She didn't like the way her husband looked. She hated to see him pushing himself so hard, sacrificing so much for them.

Letting out a big breath that was too much like another sigh, Colleen turned back to the kitchen sink and dunked the skillet into a pan of hot, soapy water. She would double down on her efforts. She'd try harder to make life go easier for Daniel—his home life, which was the only thing she could control.

And she silently vowed again not to hassle her husband.

After finishing with cleanup, Colleen lifted Scotty from his booster seat. "Let's go get ready, pumpkin. Grandpa and Nana are waiting for us."

Before she left the kitchen, Colleen looked once more at the man she'd married with such joy only four years earlier. Daniel stared at his plate of food. He'd hardly eaten a thing.

~

Saturday Afternoon
Heritage Springs, Kentucky

SCOTTY SCOOTED OFF his mother's lap and ran after the soccer ball Rob tossed across the grass. Kelly Scott's grandson had changed from a toddler into a little boy almost overnight.

She smiled as she lifted a frosty glass of lemonade and sipped the cold liquid from a straw. She loved her two guys so much. Her husband Rob was turning into a wonderful grandfather. He would have been a wonderful father too, if she had given him a chance to be. She set the glass down on the picnic table, refusing to let out a sigh of remorse.

SECRETS: BLUEGRASS HOMECOMING

The past was the past. She'd learned to let it lie. Or at least she tried not to allow guilt consume her. Kelly refused to think about "if only." Sure, she'd had choices. But at eighteen, she'd thought her options limited. If only she'd had more courage, more self-esteem, she would have spoken up—should have spoken up. If she had, maybe she wouldn't have raised her daughter Colleen as a single mom. Maybe Colleen would have known her father before she was a woman grown and married.

Kelly slid her gaze over to her daughter. They sat together on the stone patio under the shade of a canvas awning, the canopy keeping the worst of the July sun from their faces. Scotty's birthday gifts had been opened and the chocolate cake and ice cream eaten. It was good to relax a minute. Good to sit.

Her daughter was so beautiful. Colleen was tall like her father with Rob's blond good looks. She had a pert little nose and two cute dimples that appeared when she smiled. Pregnancy and childbirth had made a genuine woman out of her, rounding her figure from the slender shape of her teen years. It was nice Daniel had found a way to keep Colleen at home. His mother had been a stay-at-home mom, raising four children. Daniel made it clear he expected to do the same for Colleen and his family.

"I'm sorry Daniel couldn't make it today," Kelly said.

Colleen glanced at her mother and then quickly looked away. "He's studying."

"Yes, I know. Still, Scotty only has one three-year-old birthday party."

"Mom, don't start."

Kelly didn't want to start, but a mother's sixth sense told her something was wrong. Daniel's schoolwork had reached a crisis point six months earlier with medical school becoming a huge ordeal. At that time, he'd asked Colleen if she and Scotty could leave the house on weekends so he could study in quiet. Trying to save money and do as Daniel asked, Colleen had driven to Heritage Springs every weekend since then and stayed with Rob and Kelly.

Kelly was glad to see Scotty and her daughter so often, but her hospitality was wearing a little thin. *Darn it!* Sometimes she wanted the weekends to herself. She and Rob were almost newlyweds too. And with her husband busy during the week at his law practice, Kelly selfishly thought she didn't spend enough time with him.

But she had deprived Rob of watching Colleen grow up. For the life of her, she wasn't about to say "no" to her daughter's request. Besides, Rob got such a kick out of pretending to be Scotty's father on weekends.

Rob was with their little grandson so much he was taking the place of the child's father.

The thought jarred Kelly. Her mouth suddenly felt dry. She reached for the glass of lemonade. The bitter liquid went down her throat, cooling it, but not her annoyance. In the yard, Rob kicked the ball, and Scotty chased it, trying to mimic his grandfather and boot it back.

"It's almost five o'clock," Kelly said in what she hoped was a conversational tone as she turned her gaze back to Colleen. "If you left soon, you might surprise Daniel at home, and he'd have an hour or two with Scotty before bedtime."

Her daughter looked irritated. Kelly was interfering. But it was her prerogative, wasn't it? It came with being a mother and wanting her daughter to grow a backbone. For whatever reason, Colleen always deferred to Daniel. Kelly had tried to accept the submissiveness that had come with Colleen's relationship with Daniel. But she didn't like it one bit.

Colleen lifted her chin. "Daniel is studying."

"All day?"

"Yes. He needs the quiet time to prepare for a big exam."

Kelly returned her gaze to the backyard playing field. Rob scooped Scotty up in his arms and gave him a big hug and kiss.

"I'm glad Rob gets time to enjoy Scotty," Kelly said with a soft sigh. She swirled the lemonade in her glass. "He didn't have time with you to watch you grow up. I'm sorry Daniel is missing all this quality time with his son."

"He'll have plenty of time when he finishes med school," Colleen was quick to respond.

"Well, I hope so," Kelly said. "For Scotty's sake."

Kelly glanced at her daughter. Colleen's mouth was drawn into a thin line. Kelly recognized that look of displeasure. Whether it was with Daniel or with her suggestion, Kelly couldn't guess.

She looked toward the yard where Rob had put Scotty on his shoulders and trotted around, the child giggling and squealing with glee. No need to press Colleen. The scene in front of them told the story Kelly had tried to convey. Scotty was growing up without his real father.

Kentucky Woman

What is Jack willing to do to win the heart of this spirited Kentucky woman?

Kentucky Blue Bloods

When Kentucky blue blood tangles with British blue blood, are they willing to take a gamble on love?

Kentucky Bride / Kentucky Heat

Two novellas in one book

How far is Cam willing to go for his business? Can he turn a skittish Kentucky horse trainer into his Kentucky bride?

<>

Is Reggie crazy to think she can convince Hank he's more than just his daddy's name and fortune, without getting tangled up in his alluring Kentucky heat?

Kentucky Flame

Is there enough of an ember in the ashes of their past to reignite the flames of love?

Kentucky Groom

Can a marriage of convenience prove that a California millionaire can be the perfect Kentucky groom?

Kentucky Cowboy

Will Mandy take a second chance with her Kentucky cowboy and risk her heart this time?

Kentucky Rain

Carrying a torch is ridiculous. There's no time like the present to move on. But does Scott really want to?

Contemporary romances about second chances set in the Bluegrass of Kentucky that can be read as standalone novels with happily ever after endings and no cliffhangers.

THE MONTANA MCKENNAS SERIES

You might also enjoy a trip the a dude ranch in
The Montana McKennas series

The Prequel by Jan Scarbrough and Maddie James
Brody by Jan Scarbrough
Callie by Maddie James
Parker by Maddie James
Mercer by Jan Scarbrough
Liz by Jan Scarbrough

THANK YOU!

For purchasing this book from
Saddle Horse Press